good deed rain

I walked every sidewalk, studied every yard, and tried every door. I don't think I really knew this town until I started buying it for Mars.

GOODWIN PLENTY © 2025
Allen Frost, Good Deed Rain
Bellingham, Washington
ISBN: 979-8-3484-9279-3

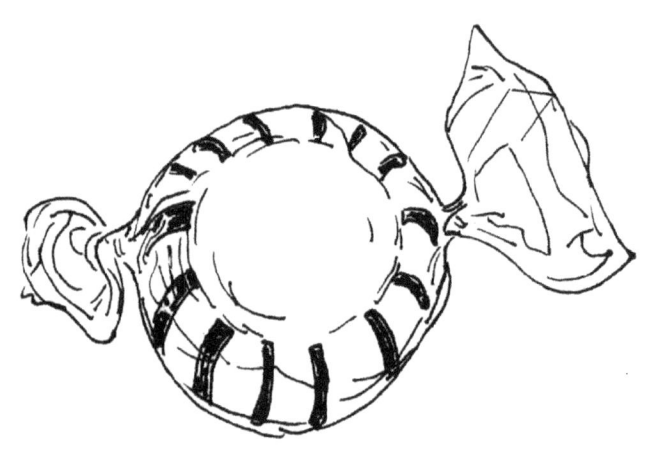

Writing, Cover & Drawings: Allen Frost
Cover Production: Robert Millis
Quote: *Munich Manual of Demonic Magic*, 15th Century, from *Forbidden Rites*, translated by Richard Kieckhefer, The Pennsylvania State University Press, 1998.
Apple: TFK!

GOODWIN PLENTY

Allen Frost

Good Deed Rain ◊ Bellingham, Washington ◊ 2025

INTRODUCTION

Early this summer, my son and I were walking past a big Spanish-style house on 24th Street and I stopped to chat with the girl in the driveway. I asked her if she knew about the history of the place, it looks like it traveled here from 1920s Hollywood. She didn't know about that, but she told me someone from a television show bought the backyard. At least that was my impression. And that brings up all kinds of possibilities for a novel. This is one of them.

—AF, August 6, 2024

CHAPTERS

Pretending	17
The Map of the City	19
Dogs	22
The Haunted Piano	24
At Home with the Plentys	27
Mermaid Laundry	31
Calypso	34
Birds	37
Ocean	41
Horsefeathers	44
The Parking Lot Appreciation Society	47
A Sunny Day on their Planet	51
Geraldine Claire	54
City View Balloon Repairs	57
Subtitles	60

Good News	63
A Hundred Million Miles from Maple Street	67
Ukeleles	70
Dreaming of Mars	73
A Circus Act	76
The Yellow Leaf	79
Good Deeds and Heroics	82
The Last Submarine Captain	85
This Precious Day	89
Every So Often	93
A Likely Story	96
The Parable of the Sheep	99
Tried and True	102
More Excitement	105
With a Caterpillar	109

A Little Jump	112
The Magic Word	115
Sky on Water	119
#34	121
Tulip	125
Beans	128
Loretta Lynn	131
Driving a Jellyfish	135
Magnified	139
A Big Dream	143
Candy	146
A Rare Ability	149
Laughs	153
Forever	156
Ever-Present	160

First go out on the tenth day of the moon, under a clear sky, outside of town to some remote and secret place, taking milk and honey with you, some of which you must sprinkle in the air.

—*Forbidden Rites*

CHAPTER ONE
Pretending

Here we go. My name is Goodwin Plenty and I work for Martians.

I know how that sounds, but jobs are hard to find in this town. I was lucky to get it. I wasn't aware of the part I would play. Let's face it, there's a lot we don't know about, right? About everything. We get by just pretending. I go to the Martian Bureau five days a week. I don't know what they're planning, but it's something worldwide. I'm not implying anything sinister from Mars. It's not like Earthlings have always been better caretakers of this planet. It's hard to ignore a long history of doing wrong and sometimes it feels like we're on our way to be gone. Empires come and go—so do dinosaurs—and with or without us the Earth will go around the sun.

I grew up here. When I was a boy I crossed Donovan Avenue to school, through the wood on the path that followed fences where the old truck farms grew patches full of greens, lettuce and cabbages, tomatoes, strawberries, blueberries, carrots, potatoes and sugar snaps. I would walk home when there were horses in the field and deer would stand in the leaves watching me. I'd roll them an apple. Wildflowers, nettles, ferns, blackberry vines, alder, cedar, oaks, ravens and maples and fir on either side of a creek. A wreck of a truck turning to rust. A deep dark forest running from town to the mountain, snow, salmon rivers and streams. In my lifetime, the stars and quiet nights got lost in the sodium haze of subdivisions and cul-de-sacs. I try not to focus on what we lost, that's the key. You can't hold onto that. It could never last. Everything is changing. We're forever dreaming. I'm in a dream right now.

With that in mind, I go to work. I keep an eye on the town, I go from street to street.

August is a good time for me. I hear a lawnmower that won't start, music to my ears, and I move right in.

CHAPTER TWO
The Map Of The City

"Hi," I said. Leaning over the fence just slightly, neighborly, I waved. I held a clipboard low in my other hand. A crowd of daisies grew through the picket fence. Most of the flowers were dry, worn out by a hot sun. "That mower's giving you trouble, isn't it?"

He stared at me.

"I bet you're pretty frustrated," I said.

"What do you think?"

I nodded. "I think you might be interested in what I have to offer. How would you like to sell off any portion of that pesky lawn so you never have to worry about upkeep ever again?" I swept my hand, "Imagine the hassle you'd avoid just having half." I shrugged, "Or none at all."

He let go of the starter cord and straightened his back. "What are you driving at?"

"I'm glad you asked. I'm prepared to pay cash for any part of your lawn."

"What?"

"Oh, believe me, you're not the only one. All over the city people are signing on."

"You want to pay me for part of my yard? How much?"

"Whatever part of it you're willing to part with."

"No—how much will you pay me."

I told him our going rate and watched his eyes turn from shock to laughter.

He said, "I can't believe it."

"I assure you, we're on the level."

"How much for that corner, say five-by-five?"

I gave him a number.

"Cash?"

"That's right." I had him on the line. This is what the Martians pay me for.

"Fine with me," he grinned. He went to the gate and let me into the backyard. I added his name and address on my clipboard. I paid him off in crisp bills. Then I measured the square that now belonged to Mars and marked the territory with red paint.

He watched me do that and finally he wondered. "What are you going to do with it?"

"Nothing at the moment. We'll keep an eye on it though. If you can get that mower to work on your property, we'll send someone to make sure that our section matches the rest of your yard."

He was dazed then he looked at the money in his hand again and it was enough for him not to wonder anymore.

I had what I needed too. It would be alarming to see the map of the city with all that consists of Mars. I don't show that around. I don't want people to get the wrong idea. For years too much has been said about Martian invasion. The newsstand pulp, the radio, the drive-in movies and television sets prepared us for the Martians to arrive. They were already here before they were here.

CHAPTER THREE
Dogs

I spoke with the manager of Stanford Apartments. He sold me a little plot on the concrete next to the garbage cans. Not much, but the Martians want whatever they can get. It was good at growing moss under the dripping rainspout. Then I hooked a right on 19th and turned onto Harris Avenue. I made conversation with a woman walking her dog and as a joke I suggested buying some space on her terrier. Wouldn't that be something? "My dog is 20% Martian," she could tell friends. I bought another spot underneath a plastic swimming pool. An inch of water treacled around the edges. The seller warned me the pool hid a hole where their dog liked to dig. I guess that doesn't matter, I'm not sure what the Martians have in mind, they just told me to gather land. I didn't ask at the fire department. It's best not to raise suspicion with city officials. The Our Savior Church accepted a hundred-dollar donation for a parcel at the corner of their parking lot on 18th. I could have carried it back to the Martian Bureau in a shovel. After I gave away all the money I had, I was done for the day. The clipboard was a page longer. All the land that nobody has thought twice about remains overlooked until it's added up.

Birds were singing above the sidewalk. Some kid left a hopscotch skeleton drawn beside my feet. Ten chalk squares. If I had any more money I could make an offer. The birds moved up and down in the tree.

I turned around and started walking home.

It was still sunny, but you could tell even the sun was tired out from the long day. It sat up in the leaves caught like an orange. The rooftops burned. I didn't have far to go. The Plenty house will be appearing soon. The Plenty family is my wife Penny, Shelley, Orville, and me. Oh, also our dog, Humbug. Orville has a goldfish too. Slowly it swims back and forth.

CHAPTER FOUR
The Haunted Piano

Humbug was waiting for me on top of the roof. I was a couple blocks away, but I could see her up there like a weathervane. I don't know how she does what she does. She's quite peculiar. As if pushed by the wind, she turned in my direction.

The haunted piano on the corner across the street was playing. We can thank Lexington Brown for that. Somehow he conjured a ghost piano and fastened it to the concrete, good for a few songs before it melts back into air. It always appears at this time, it seems to know that people are coming home from a long day at work, walking like me with home in view. It wants to please us. Some real stars have appeared at this piano too. Nina Simone. Mozart, I think. Yesterday was Thelonius Monk. Once I tried to talk to a girl playing Satie, but I went right through. We never know who will be at the keyboard. Today sounds like Fats Waller. It is—I can see his dim form, his bowler hat, confessing, "I'm the world's most happiest creature." I don't know where this music comes from. Is there a place we can't see? Is there a certain cloud that floats overhead where musicians wait on a station platform with tracks running into tunnels connected to the ground? Do they load a piano onto that ghost subway train? That's how I imagine it. I don't have to ask Lexington how it works, all that matters is it does.

The corner has become ordinary in our neighborhood, where rain or shine, every workday of the week ends when the ghost train drops off a piano and someone to play it, then picks them up again when we have reached home.

Humbug barked.

word around the house

CHAPTER FIVE
At Home With The Plentys

Really, there's nothing humbug about her, Orville picked up on that name watching *The Wizard of Oz*. He must have been three or four when he started using that word around the house and he stuck it on our Martian dog when we got her. She was a gift from the Bureau after I passed my probation. She sat under the table while we ate dinner.

"Aren't you hungry, dear?" Penny asked Shelley.

The plate next to our daughter was getting cool. Shelley wrote a word in her notebook, underlined it, tore the page free and held it in the air to read.

"Well…" Penny said. "Spaghetti is all we have tonight. Unless you want to make a sandwich."

Shelley sighed. She crossed her arms. She was done with speaking. She vowed silence from now on, it was only written words held overhead.

"I can make you one of my famous sandwiches," I said. A long second followed. What famous sandwiches? You won't hear their praise on Nat King Cole's "Route 66" piano. She didn't buy it either.

She quickly scribbled and the sentence word-ballooned above the table.

"What's it say?" asked Orville.

I read the teenage billboard aloud: "You don't understand."

With a final huff, Shelley pushed back her chair and stormed off.

"It's not easy being Martian," I said softly.

Penny pressed her finger to her lips hushing me.

"Dad needs to be quiet," Orville said.

I nodded and pretended to zipper my mouth.

"Give me the key," Orville said, holding out his cupped hands.

I tossed an invisible key across the salad bowl. He caught it and put it in his striped shirt pocket.

"She had a hard day at school," Penny said.

I pointed at myself and mimed my fingers walking to her room.

"You better leave her alone for a while."

We're all growing up in this strange world today and it isn't easy. Shelley's walls were painted desert orange to match the color of a planet a hundred million miles away. When I go in there later, I'll be an astronaut trying to make peaceful contact. I'll bring her a dish of blueberries from Earth and if she lets me, I'll give her a hug.

Penny said, "The washing machine is definitely broken."

I rolled my eyes and clutched my hands in pantomime.

"I called the repairman," she continued and she told me what he said it would cost.

I groaned, "Oh no!"

"Dad!" Orville scolded me.

"I'll go to the Bureau tomorrow," I said. "I'll ask for a loan."

Orville held my imaginary key pinched in his hand, "You can't talk yet!"

"If we want to wear clean clothes tomorrow," Penny said, "we need to go to the laundromat tonight."

I bit my lip. Orville was watching me like a hawk.

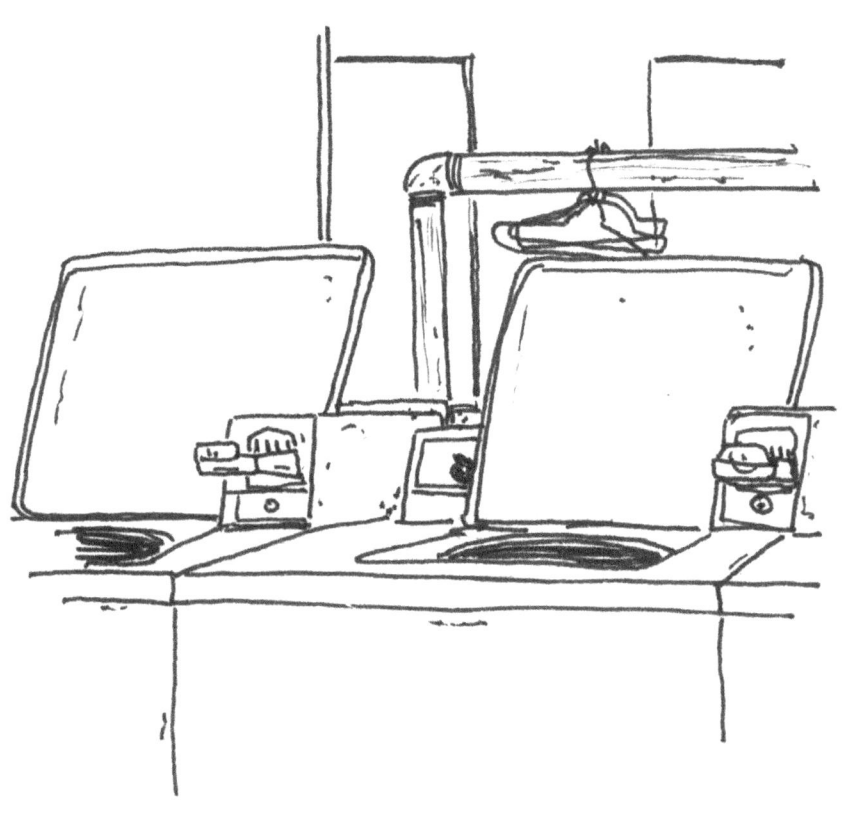

poverty churches

CHAPTER SIX
Mermaid Laundry

I like laundromats. After Penny and I married, we rented a two-room house on Grant Street. We went to the plaza laundromat every week. We had our little blue car, flower decals on the side, the backseat full of clothes in bags and a baby seat.

Shelley didn't want to come with us tonight. She told us through her shut door. Humbug kept her company.

We have a different car now. Our blue car finally broke down and probably got stamped into some unrecognizable other metal thing. Those trips to do laundry with coins we had to dig from pockets and cushions, leftover change from the poverty churches of dollar stores, Goodwill, Safeway, Social Services. Thanks to Mars we don't worry the same way, but some old prayers don't go away. Food, clean clothes and shelter.

As I drove, Orville returned my key so Penny and I could talk. The laundromat is between a pizza shop and a hardware store. The aroma of dough and sauce mixes with detergent smell next door and gets wrenched into the True Value aisles and hung with the plumbing supplies.

I got a laundry basket from the trunk while Orville ran ahead to the glass door. He likes it here too. He has his own reason. He was already inside. Penny held the door for me. The Vandellas are on the radio. I said hi to the woman at the counter. Long white hair. An air of mystery. At least I think so. I pretend she's a mermaid. As long as she's close to water she can keep her human form.

Penny opened a washing machine hatch and I set the clothes down. I remember the coin slot, three quarters used to mean a lot. We brought our own soap. There's a machine on the wall that sells single load cardboard boxes. I used to pretend they were baby shoes and put them on Shelley's feet until she kicked them free.

"I'll get the other basket from the car," I told Penny.

"Okay."

Orville was in command atop a tall red stool at a videogame machine called Moon Patrol. He holds the controls and pretends he's driving.

On the way to the door, I stopped at the gumball machines. One sells candy, the other has shiny toys. I promised Shelley I'd bring her a souvenir. I put fifty cents in and turned the handle until the bauble fell against my hand. Inside the clear ball was a silver necklace that would turn her skin green. Attached to it was a golden ankh.

CHAPTER SEVEN
Calypso

Houselights, car lights, the occasional streetlight. It was no moon buggy game. Our driveway was murky as pondwater. We stopped and Orville was on his way. He took everything at a run, across the gravel to the door, leaving Penny and me like stevedores to each take a basket to the house. Fresh clean laundry from the mermaid's lair. The moon was showing, a slice of it anyway, and I checked to see if Orville left tire tracks on it.

The excitement of warm laundry awaited, sorting, stacking, we could use some calypso from that corner piano for unloading our cargo chore. I heard Penny call for Shelley. I stopped searching the moon. I don't look at the night sky often enough. I think most of us just go along looking straight ahead.

No sooner was I inside when the door behind me tapped. I set my basket down to answer the knock. One of Shelley's friends stood on the step. She couldn't have been far from us when we arrived, but she couldn't talk. She raised a message overhead for me to read.

"Shelley's in her room," I answered her. "I can ask her. You can come in."

She stood by the door with her notebook and pen. She wrote a new message and held it up high. *I want to apologize.*

I said, "Oh, okay. That's nice." I remembered Penny said something happened at school.

Orville rode out of the kitchen on Humbug's back. He wasn't supposed to do that inside. He stopped singing loud and they turned around. I stopped at Shelley's door and rapped. "Shelley? Your friend Dinah is here. Can she talk to you?"

Dinah had a note all ready for this and she kneeled and tucked it beneath the door.

We both waited.

Whatever is happening at school, it's up to Shelley to make sense of all those mixed-up feelings and fears, stress and storylines. We can ask her questions and hope to help, but she's the one navigating the waters. I was going to say something to Dinah, I know they're friends, but I remember how that comes and goes when you're young.

A piece of folded paper pushed its way from the other side. Dinah kneeled again and quickly opened the note. I couldn't see what it said but I was relieved when she smiled. Some of the static tearing the music of the spheres had been smoothed. I didn't realize I was holding my breath until I exhaled. The handle turned and Shelley's door opened.

CHAPTER EIGHT
Birds

My clipboard! Where was it? I had it last at the mermaid's laundry. I went over figures while the machines whirled our clothes and Penny read a book and Orville was on the moon. I must have left it there. How could I?

I couldn't go to the Bureau without it. In the mornings I turn in my results. I'll admit I was in a bit of a panic. I'm not supposed to let the clipboard out of my sight. Everything will fall apart if I can't find it—I'll be fired if it's gone, we'll be on the street, I'll be begging for a place for our family to stay, one of those plots of yard I used to buy will seem a luxury. Worry, worry…

But the kids need to get to school, Penny's gone to her job. We have a daily routine. I didn't discover the clipboard dilemma until Penny drove off and work was on my mind.

Our jobs drive us crazy—we get to thinking they control our lives—it's not like Mars owns my soul. I've been poor before. Something more than money needs to be done, maybe a brand-new civilization. I got a bowl and poured some cereal. No milk, no spoon. I left it alone. I couldn't eat.

Okay, it was time to go. I almost forgot the kids' lunch before we went out the door. All I could picture was that clipboard getting into the wrong hands. What if someone brought it to the *Herald*?

I got behind the wheel of our cardboard car and started its rattling motor. Shelley sat next to me holding a backpack on her lap, notebook in her hand. When I'm driving, I can't read her words, we can't carry on a conversation, it would seem a little one-sided, like me talking to you. What does she do with all her notes anyway, keep them bunched in her bag and wait til the end of the day and make a nest of them?

What if the *Herald* does get ahold of my clipboard? What if they run a frontpage story? MARTIANS BUYING CITY. Of course I don't use the name Martian Bureau in my reports for this very reason. If someone finds my clipboard, those numbers and that map will be a mystery. Right?

"Turn on the radio!" Orville piped up behind me.

He likes the way it plays. With every bump in the road, the music changes. The dial jumps around on its own and the stations come and go like birds at a feeder. A weather report will turn into bluegrass, then opera, then something else. A cardboard car makes for a very bumpy ride. You never know what to expect. At 8 AM with a new day unfolding, we find this entertaining.

I smiled at the sound of Orville laughing. Life is in that. So what if the *Herald* discovers the clipboard? I'll think of something to say if it happens. I just need to get it back. I will. I'll stop by the laundromat as soon as the kids are delivered to school.

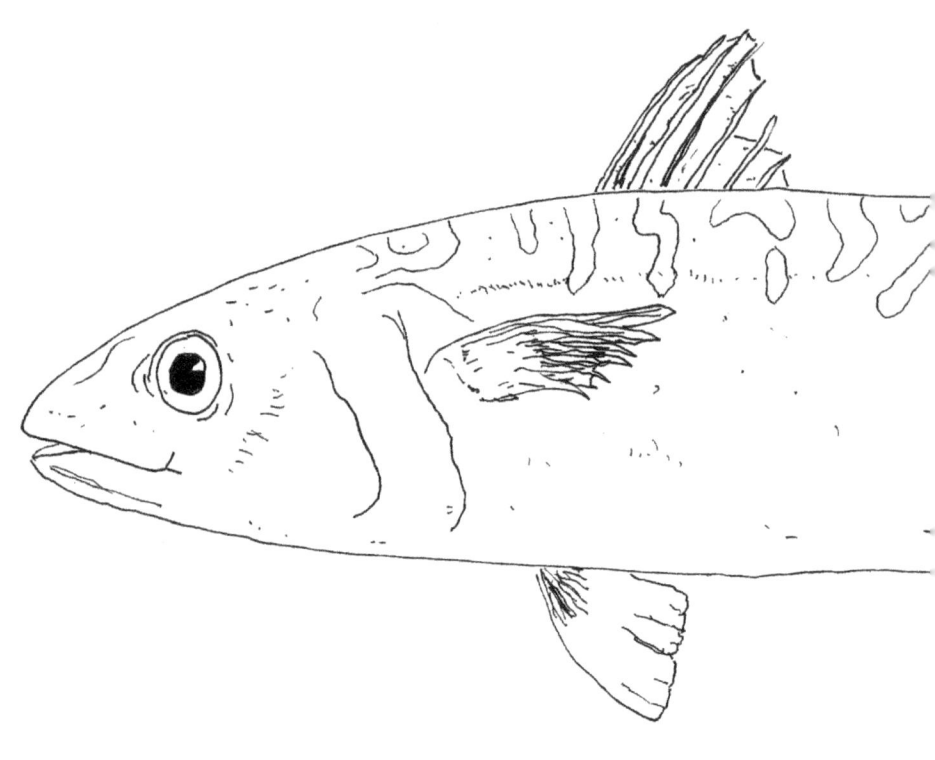

swimming lessons

CHAPTER NINE
Ocean

The same white-haired woman was at the counter. A man sat rumpled in the orange chair by the window. Tired. It was early.

"Hi," I greeted her. Did she spend the night here? Could she? Was there a backroom with a barrel full of seawater? I thought of swimming pools and swimming lessons and all the water running underground in pipes and streams and collected in aquifers.

She said, "Good morning."

"I was here last night. I think I left my clipboard. I hope I did."

She settled her elbows on the counter. Her blue eyes opened wide and I went swimming in. At first I saw ocean, swells then waves, and down I went, fish scattering like dimes, at a slant with the fading light, a whale, shipwrecks and reefs. There is so much ocean I could go a long time seeing nothing, traveling like a ghost in black emptiness, deeper and deeper into the darkness of an outer space night. These were her eyes. I was nearly drowned before she blinked and poured me out.

I was back in a laundromat.

She reached below the counter. "Is this it?"

It was.

She said, "People forget things here all the time."

"Thank you." I had it again. My worries were just sand dollars washed up on a beach.

She said, "I saw you writing in it. You seemed so serious. I was wondering what it could be."

"I'm making notes," I said. It's what I would have told the *Herald*. "For a book I'm writing."

"Will we be in it?" the man at the window croaked. I didn't know he was listening. The place was quiet. The machines were asleep. I guess I was the radio.

"Sure," I said. "Everyone's in it. Everywhere I go and everything I experience." I clutched the clipboard, just so thankful to have it back, holding it up in the air like Shelley with a note. "What I'm feeling right now will be the perfect ending for a chapter."

CHAPTER TEN
Horsefeathers

I couldn't wait any longer to give the clipboard a good look, to make sure the pages were all there and nothing strange had been added by the mermaid, like barnacles, fish scales, or a pirate's treasure red X on the map. I pulled into the first parking lot I found on Holly Street. There was a wooden-sided building in the middle of it, anchored like a ship with an ocean of paving around it. A sign on the pavement edge read: Charleston Reese Unreal Estate. I've heard of it. I had my choice of spots, there weren't any other cars. I stopped the car and got the clipboard.

I tried to see it through her mermaid eyes as she must have tried to make sense of it. Most of the writing is in code. Some of it isn't, there are some random shopping lists and reminders. It's meant to look like I've been jotting nonsense. Some fake predictions and weather reports. It could almost be mistaken for a sort of *Farmer's Almanac*. Until you see the map. I guess that would be suspicious. Little dots placed around town followed by three pages of code.

"Excuse me sir." A woman addressed me from the other side of my cardboard car.

I said, "Hello."

"Did you make an appointment?"

"No."

"This parking lot is for customers only. See…" she pointed at the signs posted along the property line.

I read the warnings on the leaning wooden fence. A huge chestnut tree. It was a glorious sight clouding over the lot. The leaves were filled with chestnuts. They'd sound like muskets cracking on the empty tar.

"What's he doing?" a man appeared in the window with her. "What do you think you're doing?" he asked me.

It was Charleston Reese himself—I've seen him in commercials.

I answered, "What am I doing? Nothing really."

"Well, you better leave. This is private property."

Then it came to me. I could've driven off, but I couldn't help myself. This was a game. Being a salesman, your mind has to be sharp as a tack. I was up for the challenge. "Actually, what I'm doing is looking for the perfect parking lot."

"Horsefeathers."

"What? No, Mr. Reese, it's true. Look," I turned the pages of the clipboard to the map and flashed it. "It's my quest. I've been looking all over town for a place like this. You've made my day! I'm going to enter your parking lot in our directory." I told him about The Parking Lot Appreciation Society and our many sponsors and all the good we do.

CHAPTER ELEVEN
The Parking Lot Appreciation Society

Some people wouldn't look twice at the unreal estate agency. It was one of those buildings that used to be a different store. I can't remember what. A radio repair? To some people, this might seem an unremarkable parking lot, cracking tar dumped over a slant. Faded yellow painted lines. Forgettable. All it had going for it was that it was empty, and it had a nice tree. The birds liked it, they were singing in it.

I agreed with them, I was actually starting to like the parking lot too. The cracking tar gave it character. The sun was lost in the green tree. I want to come back once a week. I want to watch the lot throughout the seasons. I want artists to make it famous. I want school fieldtrips to visit here. I want to see the town council make it a historical sight and sell postcards to the tourists.

I liked Charleston and I liked Ruth. She apologized and was all smiles. Charleston hiked back to the store to get a camera and when Ruth asked me if I really meant it when I said their parking lot would be featured in our calendar for July, it hurt to lie.

We waited another minute before Charleston reappeared with a camera around his neck. "You ready?" he asked me. Ruth eased away. Charleston wanted a picture of me standing in their parking lot.

"Okay, Charleston," I said. I smiled at the camera, that was easy, thinking how glad I was to have my clipboard back. Finding it sent me here like following a treasure map. I don't know what the Bureau would do if I lost this clipboard. If the mermaid knew what I left at her laundromat, what I took away, she didn't let on or falter. All the water that rushed around her machines kept her steady on land and alert enough to care for the lost and found.

Charleston brought the camera down and said,

"That's a good one." He and Ruth seemed awfully kind, the sort of small-town folks that once were plentiful here. Their unreal realty sold people imaginary places. They could install a picture wall in your apartment that matched your perfect world. It felt like you were there, wherever you wanted to be moved in real time while hidden speakers and ducts matched the air there. We never had that machinery installed in the Plenty house. If you read Ray Bradbury, you'll know why. These days, ordinary people can't afford their services anymore, their business must be desperate for attention and any dollar they can get. The parking lot was their welcome mat. Or spiderweb. Too bad I wasn't a housefly.

Charleston said, "I tell you what. You give me ten dollars and I'll get the photo developed for you. Ruth will put it in a nice frame. Come by next week and get it."

I searched my pocket. "All I have is a five. And some ones."

"That's fine." He didn't mind. He quickly took what I had.

"Okay," I said, "I'll see you in a couple weeks."

"Bye now," said Ruth.

I returned to my car. The engine rattled. I glanced into the mirror. They waved at me as I steered into Holly traffic.

CHAPTER TWELVE
A Sunny Day On Their Planet

Sometimes I stop at the 7-Eleven to get coffee before work. I did that today. I got out of the car and almost walked inside before I realized I gave Charleston all my money. Circus ringmaster P.T. Barnum is credited with saying there's a sucker born every minute. I carried my minute under my arm like an albatross. It dawned on me that Charleston and Ruth hooked me from the beginning. I bet his camera didn't even have film! I got played…I don't know why the Martians picked me to be a salesman. Then again, the clipboard is filling up, right? I can't win them all, nobody can, still it hurt to find that out. In future I would avoid places like Charleston Reese Unreal Estate.

I turned right on Meridian Street. I found parking in front of the Asia Market. I keep some quarters for meters. I opened the ashtray and got 50¢. Outside, I tucked the clipboard under my arm with the albatross.

The Martian Bureau was next door, between the market and Better Vacuums. There's no sign on the red storefront. The bamboo window shade is always down. I entered my code and opened the door. The handle is cold, worn brass. They keep the light inside at a soft dim. Apparently it replicates a sunny day on their planet. I shut the door. In the center of the gloom is a table, in front of a curtain that runs across a doorway. The floor is covered in sand. My shoes hushed in it.

I stopped at the table and said hi to the robot. It's about the size of a slot machine, set on the tabletop like a paperweight. Its eyes are blinking red. I handed over my clipboard and it started reading. While it computes the information, I stand there awkwardly and look at the green curtains. I've never seen what's behind them. Mysterious.

"You have done well, Goodwin Plenty."

"Thanks." What a relief! The robot stamped the clipboard and gave it back to me with more money in the envelope. Then I remembered Penny and I discussing the washing machine and the leaking kitchen sink and how our car needs a new heatshield and—there seems to be a never-ending list. Oh, the vacuum cleaner also, we need it repaired. I asked the robot for a loan.

CHAPTER THIRTEEN
Geraldine Claire

Another day at the mill. I did alright. There were new red dots on the map. It was overcast when I got done, when I drove towards home. The radio bumped to a new station. "Attention, if any unknown person attempts to purchase your property contact your nearest security official." I turned the radio off. Almost there. I slowed the cardboard car when I saw the corner piano.

A familiar ghost wasn't playing it, I stopped because something was wrong.

The ghost looked like a woman from an old silent film. You don't see people in clothes like that. She wasn't sitting at the piano, she was turned towards the street, she was staring at me, but I don't know if she was seeing me.

I opened the car hatch and approached her.

She said, "Where am I?" Getting lost in time must be terrible.

Could I help her? As far as I'm aware you can't talk with a ghost. Can you talk to a cloud? Once a ghost is uncorked, who knows what can happen.

"Who are you?" she asked me.

"My name's Goodwin. I live across the street."

"How did I get here?"

"I don't know. But don't worry, I don't think you'll last long."

She sat down on the piano bench. She looked down the street, waiting for the ghost train to take her to the next station. "My name's Geraldine Claire," she told me. "What year is this?"

I told her and it didn't seem to surprise her. This was a dream she was dreaming. She folded her hands on her lap.

"Do you play piano?" I asked.

"Oh, a little. Where I'm from everyone plays a little piano."

"Can you play something? I think that's why you're here."

"I can try." She swung around and faced the piano keys. The song was familiar. It was one of those Tin Pan Alley tunes. I knew where it was going, and when she started to sing I could see another world, tall lanky tenements and laundry lines, coal fired chimneys, open windows, pianos here and there, before radio and neon and cars, where I would've been a ragman giving way to the milkcart pulled by horses. Her voice was like a violet. Then, in the quick space of a blink, where all the world goes dark for a microsecond, she and the music vaporized.

It was ten past six.

I'm still here in the future, going back to a cardboard car.

CHAPTER FOURTEEN
City View Balloon Repairs

I'm not the only person in town working for Martians. Although they try to keep us apart, scheduling our Bureau arrivals at different hours to avoid contact, I met Hector by accident one morning. He was holding what looked like an inflatable lifeboat, crumpled canvas all wound up with rope. Maybe it was a giant deflated yo-yo? He knocked with his shoe. The robot wasn't answering the door for him. I don't know if it can, I've never seen it leave the tabletop.

I said hello. I'm sure other people stop at the Martian's door. It's intriguing, no sign, what is it? Another salesman or peddler like me might leave a pamphlet stuffed in the jamb. I asked him if he needed help.

"I entered my door code, but it's not working."

A truck full of tin cans slowly shook past on the street. I almost had to shout to talk. It turned out we both worked for the Bureau.

"They gave me this to live in," he told me.

Of course! His house was a balloon. They're cheaper than an apartment and the view is something else. They grow sparsely around like dandelions above the roofs and trees, safe from telephone lines. I asked him what happened to it.

He let it drop to his feet. He took off his glasses and ran his sleeve over his face. It couldn't be easy lugging that house around in the sunshine. "It popped. I think one of my customers did it."

I commiserated. "They wanted their land back?"

He shrugged. A salesman's life isn't the romantic pilgrimage you've heard about. Most people shut you out right away and a few of them get mean. Sometimes dogs bark at you, sometimes people. "I'll see if my code works," I said.

It did. I held the door open for him as he scooped up his house and went into the dim.

The robot gave a surprised chirp when it saw both of us.

Hector approached the table and let the house

fall on the sand. He explained what happened. The robot listened, red eyes glowing. I don't think it was anger, they're always that way. Hector begged for a loan for a new balloon. Later on, I'd be asking for a loan too. When you live paycheck to paycheck there's not much room for disasters. The robot clicked and whirred and compromised. It gave him the address of City View Balloon Repairs and just enough money to pay them for a patch and a reseam.

    I don't know how many of us work for the Martians. We have our separate routes, we cover the ground and get home tired at night.

CHAPTER FIFTEEN
Subtitles

What about these Martians, anyway? They're nothing like the movies. Except for the antenna, you'd never know they're from Mars. Oh, and they have an odd way of talking. They can't speak, their words go up in the air and stick there for you to read like subtitles in a French movie. I've never seen a Martian at the Bureau—they might stay behind that green curtain—but we see them around town. They smile and enjoy Earth. They don't seem bothered by the state of things or the news on our radios. For them, every day is something new and wonderful. You have to admire that. We're used to believing the world can't be helped, there's too much greed and ignorance. It's nice to believe that's not true.

Shelley wants to be Martian. She's not the only one, there are clubs at school, events where they get together with their notebooks and paper words fluttering. She's saving her money to visit Mars. That's her dream. The pictures on her wall and the music she plays, I feel like she's already halfway there. Penny and I are putting a little money aside too. We want to surprise her when we have enough for a roundtrip ticket. If it's her dream, we have to do everything we can.

I'll tell you one thing though: she goes through a lot of notebooks! On the seat was a new one from the Grocery Outlet. Also, a couple bottles of Ukrop's Artificial Orange juice for her and her brother. I used to tell the kids it came from Mars. At 59¢ it was a bargain treat. Penny would make a face, but I also had one of those apple pies they make in a factory.

On the skyline to the south, through a gap in the trees, I could see a couple balloons. I wondered if one of them was Hector's. Penny and I considered a balloon a long time ago when we got married. We even climbed a rope up into a show model. Suddenly two people living in a balloon far over the streets didn't seem so economical or appealing.

I'm glad for our house.

Besides, Shelley was on the way. A baby in a balloon could float away. That sort of thing happens.

Penny will be overjoyed to hear the Bureau gave us a loan. On top of the clipboard is a two-dollar bouquet of flowers and a dark chocolate bar. I went a little crazy at the Outlet. I didn't even use food stamps. Sometimes a celebration is in order.

I parked the cardboard car, I was home.

CHAPTER SIXTEEN
Good News

Astronauts tell us how much they love and miss this world when they're floating in outer space.

I heard a dog a couple yards from here. Some crows cawed in line in flight. A car parked down the street, turning off its headlights. The radio tower on top of the Leopold waved a red lantern. Higher in the sky, a bright distant planet or a star. It wasn't an ordinary end of day. I was holding onto my precious clipboard balanced with these little presents. I used my knee to shut the cardboard hatch. I couldn't leave the car outside, not if there was rain later on, but the weather looked okay. A few purple clouds. The stars would start showing up in the rest of the sky.

Before I got to the door, Shelley pushed it

open. Her excitement was crayoned around her. She almost spoke by accident. I know she wants to be Martian, but I miss the sound of her voice. She started writing fast. Light came from the house. I could hear Orville riding his wooden bike, to the kitchen probably.

Shelley waved her note above her head waiting for me to read it, on her toes, almost hopping. We were close, whatever it was that had her so excited was spelled in the air like Times Square.

I read the note. "You have to go?" I love her handwriting, I guess that will be her new voice. "Go where?" As long as it isn't Mars, I'm not ready for her to leave.

She dug into her sweater pocket and unfolded a flyer. Up it went held by both her hands.

"Are these bands?" I asked.

She made such a face I had to laugh. I know they are—she knows I know they are.

She wrote another note. She blocked the doorway, dinner was waiting, so was I. She was well aware I would say yes to just about anything to get inside.

I leaned in to read it. "Well, if your mom says okay, I guess we can go."

Shelley doesn't often get like this, she used to when she was little, when simple things like a ladybug or winning tic-tac-toe would please her. She hugged me tightly and I almost dropped everything as she ran inside to tell Penny her good news.

up like a rocket

CHAPTER SEVENTEEN
A Hundred Million Miles From Maple Street

The Karate Church steeple kicks straight up at the nighttime sky. We hiked up Maple Street in the dark, Shelley hurrying ahead of us, Orville jumping in and out of the houselights cast on the sidewalk. The white steeple was lit up like a rocket, a painted banner stretched over the doorway: MARTIANS WELCOME! The music was already playing—we're a little late getting here—Shelley had to dress just right. Then there was Orville. He's wearing his Sand Lion costume. That was still his favorite animal, a Martian creature that lives a hundred million miles from Maple Street.

The last time I was here I bought a three-by-ten portion of their yard, a flying carpet of burdock and dirt. Colored lights flashed in the Gothic windows. Fifty years ago, the old church became a short-lived karate school. The name stuck. The black dragon is still painted on the siding. These days the church is trying to get by hosting events like tonight. They could use the money the Bureau provided. Funny that Mars now owns a part of this. Shelley's red dress flowed under the Martians Welcome banner. Her brother hopped on the stones along the path, growling and pawing at a moth.

Two girls ran around us. They wore Martian clothes too. One of them held to her antenna as it wobbled like a halo. "A Sand Lion!" they laughed around Orville. At the same time, they clapped their hands over their mouths. They forgot to say that with notebooks.

"Hurry up!" Orville called back at us. He wasn't waiting, his tail was wagging.

Penny and I were dressed like Earthlings. We were a little slower than them, it must have been the gravity. Music and flashing lightbulbs. Kids filled the church. They have made being Martian their own thing, happy in here in handsewn clothes or birthday gifts from astronauts, hands in the air, with foil antennas, holding up lyrics they all know by heart.

Penny squeezed my hand as she looked around us. It was like walking in a museum with a girl. The best part was watching her. It was Mars made of paint and crayons and cutout cardboard and streamers. We don't get out together much, unless you count shopping or the laundromat and back and forth with the kids. I squeezed her hand in reply. I remembered this feeling we were revisiting. Music for young people is especially magic. When I was Shelley's age, it was The Belateds that got me going like a spinning top. I knew all about them, I heard interviews on the radio, kneeled before the TV when they were on, their records lined my shelf and wore themselves into scratches as they got me ready for every day and what life lay in store.

CHAPTER EIGHTEEN
Ukeleles

The next morning was Saturday and it was raining. Penny was curled up dreaming under the covers like a comma. The house was sleeping. I went to the kitchen and poured water in a pot.

Penny and I met in a café. She was a waitress. I was a dishwasher. Shakespeare was watching. I would get there in the morning when four big pots of water were boiling potatoes for the breakfast rush. The blue gaslit fires under them. I remember Penny wrote a note and taped it over the sink for me. In those days we used to sleep in two sleeping bags zipped together, listening to Hawaiian LPs. Ukeleles led us here. A long voyage to this early morning.

I cut five potatoes and sent them to sea in the

water. They ought to be ready when Humbug and I get home from our walk.

Miraculously, the rain stopped when I opened the door. For the moment. We crossed the wet street. My sandals squeaked. I glanced at the piano corner just in case Geraldine was back. Nope. Humbug pulled my arm ahead. It wouldn't be long before she floated off the ground and I'd be pulling on a balloon dog.

On the other side of the street, the cement thumbed aside and the soil patches, making a ragged weedy path. It would be a good bit of property for Mars if I knew who to buy it from. We hopped off the road. Humbug knows the way. She was walking on only two legs by the time we reached the blackberries. I stopped so we could pick some. They'd be good with breakfast. Humbug ate some growing low to the ground, rising slowly to reach higher ones. I didn't bring anything to carry my handful, I could only put berries in my coat pocket.

After my pockets were full, I said "come on" and Humbug floated off the vines. The leaves shook from her turbulence. The rain left the path spongy. I could tell rain was coming back soon,

I didn't want to go far. My shoes were quacking again. I stepped around a slug. This is their kind of weather. When it's sunny, it's the Sand Slugs turn to crawl. Rockets from Mars brought them here in cargo holds and they adapted. Humbug blimped. I started thinking again about those old Penny days. After my late-night shift at the café, I followed the maze of dark neighborhood streets picking flowers for her and filling my pockets and when I got to Penny's house I would go in through the kitchen and up the stairs to her room. A creaky old rooming house. Her bedroom would be blue and underwater-looking. When we came together everything changed. We rented houses, we had babies, we had good and bad adventures, we had different jobs until I found the one with Mars and things got easier.

    I turned around where a creek broke across the trail. All that rain has to go somewhere. It would run like a train until the last drop, a boxcar carrying a thimble of rain. The sun would return. The ground would dry and the creek would leave itself imprinted like a fossil.

CHAPTER NINETEEN
Dreaming Of Mars

Orville was watching Muttley on TV. A cartoon dog flying a cartoon plane. Our dog Humbug was airborne too, walking along the ceiling. I could hear Humbug chuffing. Orville taught her to laugh like that cartoon dog. We hear it quite often, usually at my expense.

I carried a breakfast plate from the kitchen. Muttley's cartoon airplane was zigzagging like a butterfly. So was Humbug, just missing the ceiling light. I had to duck. Penny sat on the couch with blackberries and a cup of tea. She poured a cup for me. Shelley was still asleep in her room. She could go on all morning, dreaming of Mars. I wondered if she talked in her dreams, or was she followed everywhere by notes. Once I asked her about an invention I thought of. A little billboard she could wear atop a hat perhaps. She could type words and they'd appear on the hat screen. Her face was answer enough to that. I put the idea away behind a mental door that wouldn't be opened again. I have other furniture in that dark room, piled around a rocking chair memory moving by itself like a pendulum. I set the plate on the coffee table in front of Orville, sat beside Penny and we watched television with our hungry Sand Lion.

After Monday, Tuesday, Wednesday, Thursday, Friday, this was all I wanted to do. Relax in our house while Saturday morning rain salted the windows. "We got back just in time," I said. The summer weather was coming to an end. The two-dollar flowers stared at the room from a glass jelly jar by the teapot. Orville laughed out some potatoes and Humbug chuckled over us. I said, "When I was at the grocery yesterday, the cashier said he didn't want it to rain. I said I didn't mind it. He said everyone tells him they're glad for the rain. But he wants to be somewhere it's sunny all the time."

Penny blinked. "I guess it would be hard to have to talk about the weather all day. And each person is only there long enough to pay."

"You know what I told him?"

"Hmm?"

"I said, I've heard good things about Mars." Humbug chuckled at me. Mars is an awful long way to go to get away from the rain.

CHAPTER TWENTY
A Circus Act

How did the Martians find me? Of all things, it was at the Saturn Circus. Thanks to a fortunetelling machine. We were just three then, me and Penny and Shelley. Orville was somewhere in the invisible future. Shelley drew us into a tent full of fairground games. No wonder—she was lured by all the blinking neon-colored lights and the stuffed toys hanging from the beams. I tried to win her a bear and threw four dollars down the carnival drain. Penny won her first try and Shelley stopped crying the second she had the bear in her arms. We could have been a circus act. On the way out of the tent I stopped at a machine called Fortune Teller. Actually—now that I think about it—it looked very similar to the robot at the Mars Bureau. That's strange…I never thought about that before…I suppose it's possible. The robot wouldn't be difficult to disguise. This one looked like it had been in the circus a long time. I remember the tarnished, scarred metal. The red chipped paint on it. I put a quarter in and turned the dial. It turned reluctantly until the coin stuck out of sight in gears as old as a Hudson Terraplane. A paper card dropped into a tray. My fortune.

Go to 2309 Meridian for a job interview.

That was pretty specific.

Suspiciously so, I thought, but Penny convinced me to at least go look at the address.

You can imagine what I thought when I first saw the outside of Mars Bureau. Beat-up, anonymous, dumped on the sidewalk. And that was ten years ago, since then time has passed and sanded it more. You'd never guess there was a robot from another planet inside.

At that time, I was working in a canning factory. It was easy for me to answer the Martian's offer. I had a week of paid training before they hired me. They gave me a clipboard. My first job was watching a puppet show. I rode my bike to the June on the Moon Children's Theater under the Aurora

Bridge. I had to write a five-page essay about "The Princess and the Pea." I don't know why, or what happened to my review after the robot took it from me. It must have been acceptable. Step one. Other odd jobs followed. I must have been doing alright. Gradually, I was working my way up and down and sideways on their corporate ladder until I reached the Department of Earth Sales and a raise. For the first time, our family wasn't trying so hard to stay afloat.

CHAPTER TWENTY-ONE
The Yellow Leaf

I don't think I really knew this town, at least South Hill, until I started buying it for Mars. Then I walked every sidewalk, studied every yard, and tried every door. It made for a long and tiring day and by the time I got near Café du Paris, I would go in for some coffee. My favorite spot was the corner, against the wall, by the window. There I got to be Jacques Tati, just watching the 14th Street movie. One day, this was last year, early autumn, I was listening to accordion and trying absentmindedly to decipher the waitress talking to the cook—I don't think it's French at all—I've heard rumors that's true, that this place just pretends to be French, but that's fine with me, they have built a dream here and they're bound to stay with it.

Across the street, a yellow leaf fell.

I sat up and leaned to get a better view. Yes, there was something over there I never noticed before. The branches did their best to hide it from me but falling leaves made windows in the tree cover like moth holes in a sweater.

I finished my coffee, left a few dollars on my table and left the café.

I couldn't spot what I thought I saw from my chair, just a dense wall of twigs. After waiting for a car, I crossed the road and hopped the curb. I had to step off the sidewalk into the brush to notice the traces of a narrow cobblestone path and in I went, pushing overgrowth aside. No point building suspense, the path ended at a soggy little lopsided house that had been sliding into shadows since 1929. Blackberry vines hung around it. A broken statue guarded the door.

It looked like a place that could really use some Martian money.

I took a step forward, as close as I dared, then I stopped. I was cold. I read books like this every night. It occurred to me this was no house, but the haunted castle in a fairytale, one like "Beauty and the Beast" where Beauty is all that is light and hopeful and she was here before but now she's long gone, and the birds of poverty have picked the place clean and if it had a last breath to beg, the wind has already taken that away.

I turned around. I didn't tell Mars. I'm not even sure the house was real.

CHAPTER TWENTY-TWO
Good Deeds And Heroics

While Shelley had breakfast, the rain stopped. Apparently. It still looked suspiciously gray out there like the rain was spying down from a cloud corner, with paratroopers lurking on tree branches waiting to jump, ready to start up the second we went outside. I wasn't going to let that stop us, no way. Saturdays and Sundays are holidays when I can forget about five days of work.

Penny laughed. She said Humbug and I were staring out the window the same way. It's true. I don't know what the dog was thinking, but I was remembering a puddle I bought—I guess I was still thinking about work after all! On another rainy day like today, I spotted the puddle as I walked alongside Taylor Avenue. To a sparrow it would've been a pond. To me it looked like a cash cow, slogged at the edge of a yard, turning the grass to a spot the owners would have to avoid when they mowed. Surely they'd be glad to let it go. I was right too, they sold it to Mars for a hundred dollars. I painted around its edges, making a corral, with cars going by and the rain on my back.

"Hey!" I said. "I just had a good idea!" I thought everyone would be staring at me the way people do when someone in a musical has something rousing to say, but Orville was watching a blue aardvark on TV, and Shelley was carefully biting a shape into her toast. Penny considered me. She gave me the time of day, as the expression goes. But all that was about to change.

Something we used to do was calling me. "I'll be right back." I left the room. We still have our uniforms somewhere, I'm sure. Humbug trotted after me, at least she could feel the crackling excitement in the air. Through the kitchen to our laundry room. Telephoning to get the washing machine repaired would have been a more practical plan. I did think that, but the Plentys needed an adventure. I hope this doesn't feel out of place in a thriller about Martians buying planet Earth, but this is our story, this is our daily life, when we're together we create our own world. I lifted the laundry basket and dug into a cardboard storage box. Winter hats, gloves and coats that didn't melt like the snowman they built. "Ahah!" I found what I was looking for.

Four navy-blue ponchos with buttons and ribbons sewn on for good deeds and heroics. Over on Samewish Avenue, there's a carwash. It's been there all these years. We used to drive over there in our imaginary machine. We've been away a long time. We get older of course but we can bring memories out of boxes and get into them again. We'll board our car like the old days and it will glide through the waves, in and out of the storm. The crew of The Samewish Submarine are ready for the water and foam, go ahead and rain on us!

CHAPTER TWENTY-THREE
The Last Submarine Captain

Okay, back to the Martians. I bet you've been waiting. A good salesman has to know his audience.

It turned out nobody wanted to go to the carwash with me. Instead, I was handed a shopping list. I saluted. Down to the sea in ships. The captain of The Samewish Submarine was all alone behind the wheel. The radio plied along the dial. Orville would have enjoyed the sound. Food Giant is only a mile away. Hard to believe there were cows and horses behind wooden fences when this road was dirt.

"How would you like a trip to Mars?" said the radio.

I turned up the volume. I didn't want the channel to change before I got the details. Fortunately, they got right to the point. All I had to do was call. I memorized the numbers by turning them into a song. I sang it aloud while I turned into a parking lot where there's a phone booth.

As I sprang from the car. I realized I was wearing my Captain uniform, singing numbers over and over. I appeared to be a nincompoop but that didn't stop me running to the phone in front of 7-Eleven. I can't say for certain this is the last telephone booth in town, I know they're getting rare. It's moments like this where my appreciation of them borders on Biblical. I grabbed the receiver and dropped a couple quarters and dialed my song lyrics.

After another ring I heard, "Hello, Caller #53."

I said, "Hello."

"Do you want a ticket for Mars?"

I said, "Yes. I mean—" I was going to say my daughter does.

"Well, you're our lucky winner!"

Maybe I'm gullible. It didn't occur to me this could be Charleston Reese all over. I told the announcer our address and he told me the ticket would arrive in the mail this afternoon. After I hung up, after I clapped my hands, I stood there in the store's reflection for a long moment. Oh, I couldn't wait to tell Shelley! But did we want her to go so soon? Penny and I put money aside, a little each week, slowly accumulating towards that goal. It certainly was a dilemma. A kid stepped outside the 7-Eleven and watched me get in the car. Later, he can tell his friends he saw the last submarine captain salute from a Buick Roadmaster.

candy

CHAPTER TWENTY-FOUR
This Precious Day

I can't figure out how she got them to do it, but Shelley and Orville wanted to help Penny make soup, although I'm certain that a bowl of chocolate chips played a part. How smart Penny is. Next time I need a crew, I'll stock the submarine with candy.

Done putting away groceries, it was a good time for me to take Humbug for another walk. I wanted to be back soon in case the ticket arrived. That was going to set off the house like a firework. Humbug led me to the door and we set off.

The path didn't look that different from this morning or yesterday or last May. I bet I could walk it blindfolded, but Humbug was seeing more than me. She never tired of it, the smells were constantly changing, the weather, the light, the texture underfoot and in the air.

We stopped for a few blackberries. There were

still a lot of good ones. Humbug was flying as we joined the path again. A bicycle rounded us fast, wheels scratching gravel, the rider ducking under the leash, saying something I didn't catch. I looked behind me in case a bear was chasing. We were safe. Pressing on through the morning, I had to hop the creek. These were the rainy days of plenty the creek would remember.

When we reached the field, I let Humbug loose. I walked in the tall grass while she ricocheted in currents above the ground. There were swallows here in July, but they were gone for the year, the sky was clear to the clouds. We weren't alone though, three kids were coming towards us, a boy and two younger girls, with their dog bounding in circles. I smiled. I waved. They waved back and we got closer.

"I've never seen a Martian dog in person," the boy said. He seemed about thirteen. The girls stayed close together and cooed and tried to touch Humbug's fur as he looped the loop. "They're a bit rare on Earth, aren't they?" he said brightly. The three of them had an air to them. I've been reading *The Lion, the Witch and the Wardrobe* to Orville at night and that was my first impression, that they pushed through an English manor house to get here.

They introduced their dog and what do you know—their dog was named Gimli from *The Lord of the Rings*. The girls wanted the dogs to play, but Humbug buzzed around us like a bumblebee, snickering when she dropped her ball and it bounced off of me.

I noticed they all carried paper milkshake cups, all nearly done, and I asked if they got them from the Snow Queen on Samewish Ave. I pictured them coming all this way by sled, pulled by Gimli.

The boy spoke for them, "Yes, it's the end of summer."

That was a surprise to me. "Is it the end? Already? When does your school start?"

"Thursday."

Was that true? Not where we're from, our kids' school started a couple weeks ago.

"We're not looking forward to going back," the taller girl said gloomily and her sister and brother agreed.

"I don't blame you," I said. I didn't want to keep them from hanging on to this precious day. They carried on. I threw a ball for Humbug. She caught it before it touched the weeds, turned and sped back to me, past me, and landed in the grass where the kids had been. There was something lying there. It was money. It must have fallen from one of their hands or pockets.

"C'mon Humbug." I ran after them, into the cover of trees. They were ahead on the path, side by side, and they all jumped as Humbug swooped.

"Hey!" I called. "Did you drop this?" Five dollars means a lot to a kid. To me it means not so much. I guess that's progress.

CHAPTER TWENTY-FIVE
Every So Often

Every so often when I'm off duty, walking the dog, or driving, I'll catch myself looking at land I could buy, and I have to remind myself this is Saturday or Sunday or some Martian holiday: I'm not at work.

I've never considered the field up for grabs. I love it the way it is. We come here every day. The swallows come here every summer from Capistrano. I thought of the three schoolkids and their dog. Apparently characters from books come here too. I was still thinking about how funny it was meeting them. I wondered if they were going to step from a wardrobe when they got home.

When I buy property for Mars, I look for places that wouldn't be missed, like a cold shadow behind a garage. I don't know what the Martians have planned, but anything they do with these bits of roots and rubble ought to be better than their current state. Maybe they'll do nothing at all, maybe they'll leave them alone, turn them into miniature national parks.

There's a view coming up, just around the next corner of leaves—here it is, in a space framed between trees. Unreal estate buildings are sowed around, they have a page in the telephone book. They're found in malls and tacked between betting shops and bodegas, and marooned in empty parking lots. Even though times are tough for the rest of us, they're making a bundle. Millionaires. You should see their yachts and mansions hidden from view. This one though is in plain sight. It deserves a moment to contemplate Magnificent Marvin's house. He lives in a fifty-foot-tall dandelion. I'm too far away to see in the windows, but he's in there somewhere. He's the king of them all. The late-night movies and detective shows are checkered with his commercials. He's one of those rare characters like Willy Wonka. I'll never forget the forest Marvin made in the parking lot of Food Giant. They kept us separated from it by a rope after a family trying to get to their station wagon was chased by wolves. It was hard to believe all those trees weren't real. So many things are strange these days. Every time I stop at this clearing, I look at the flower. A spiral staircase runs around the stem. Every so often I think this will be the day I'll see him slowly climbing it with a bag of groceries.

CHAPTER TWENTY-SIX
A Likely Story

Orville has a windup radio. A few spins and he finds the Appalachian station. Music from another world. This is his ritual every evening at bedtime.

We have made it here, a long day is over. I shut the door and fell into bed. Behind the wall, violins and guitar play in Orville's room. We called goodnight and I read a page of *Ask the Dust* before I was asleep.

Not for long though. I gave a jump as Orville woke me up.

He stood in the dark. "Artemus is back!"

"What?"

"Listen!" he poked the radio at us. We could hear a faint voice cleaving through the static.

Penny was pretending to be asleep. A likely story.

"We have to go see him, Dad! We need to go outside and look!"

"Okay…" I looked at Penny. Her eyes were closed but she was smiling.

I love Orville's excitement, but—I glanced at the green alarm clock numbers—it was 10:44. I followed him downstairs. We put on coats in the laundry room and Orville was out the door like a rabbit.

Artemus appears once in a blue moon like a comet. He can't predict when he will see our lights at night, we only know when we hear him on the radio. What a fate. He was stuck in the slipstream migrating up and down the coast with the wind, a mile above the ground in a KGUS broadcast balloon. While he was doing his program a year ago, the rope broke and there's been no way to get him down. A tragedy. It takes more than human ingenuity to retrieve him. Maybe on Monday I'll ask the Martians if they can catch him. "Careful, Orville," I called. Orville scurried onto the swing set. His shoes banged on the slide and his silhouette stared up.

"Any idea where he's coming from?" I asked when I reached him. The sky was wide.

"I'm not sure." The radio signal was getting clearer.

We both searched the night sky. A halo glow smudged over the backyard. Above it shined plenty of stars and a planet or two. The moon was mysterious as ever.

I said, "Do you remember that story about the cow that jumped over the moon? Why'd it do that?"

"It was hungry, I think. I think it wanted cheese."

Okay. That made sense. Mother Goose would be happy with that explanation.

Suddenly Orville cried, "Look! There he is!"

CHAPTER TWENTY-SEVEN
The Parable Of The Sheep

I woke up again at 3 AM. I often do. I wouldn't call it insomnia, it's my ghost o'clock. It's when haunted thoughts arrive. I know it's hopeless to worry and hang them up like wet laundry and I try not to. It took until now for me to remember we didn't receive Shelley's ticket. Did they get our address wrong? I couldn't call them back, I couldn't remember my song. It was a one-hit wonder, it got me a ticket to Mars and then it was forgotten.

I turned onto my left side towards the window. Maybe Artemus was messing with my peace of mind. A frequency in orbit. Couldn't people receive radio in their fillings? I've heard that's true. We live in an age of wonders. I moved my arm. I could see a sliver of slate-gray night between the curtains. Wait…How could I win a ticket to Mars? Passage there can only be issued by Martian authorities, with passports, stamps and immunization proof. Not only that—how could a Martian be on the radio? Martians can't talk! How could they announce contests? And why would they have telephones?

The time was 3:39. I shouldn't have looked. I stared at the ceiling instead.

It was okay, I'd fall asleep eventually. Tomorrow was Sunday, I had a whole other day off from Mars. I pulled the blanket around my shoulder. There's nothing I can do about the ticket at this hour. If it was another Charleston Reese situation and I was a sap, then so be it. I thought about the Bureau on Monday. I wondered if I could request to go back to writing puppet reviews. I was good at that.

I shut my eyes.

I pictured a sheep. It was in a field. I put another one next to it. Then two lambs next to them. That was four. I added some more and counted them. 5, 6, 7, 8. I stopped counting and made it a flock. Numbers were written on their wool. 72. 44. I saw one that was 195. What are they supposed to do, how could this help me sleep? I tried to keep them from leaving the field. The gate was open, I had to push between sheep to get to it and heave it shut. Some of them wandered on the other side. What would happen to them when I fell asleep? I'd be in a dream far away. What a catastrophe. Then I got it—it's a parable—this is why you should never fall asleep on the job.

CHAPTER TWENTY-EIGHT
Tried And True

After breakfast I watched birds from the window chair. A robin tugging at a worm. Our front yard doesn't catch the sun until later. The dew prevailed on everything for a while. I can't imagine selling a bit of our yard. We're not in the same position as a lot of people though, we're not praying for some way to make the rent or pay a hospital bill. I was about to be tested on that.

A bicycle stopped in front of our house.

"Dad," Shelley said, "what time is the thing today?"

I turned. Her antenna was askew. I said, "In a couple hours." I told her she had time, there was hot tea in the pot, she could have some. I didn't point out that she talked—it might not have been

Martian, but I was glad she did.

When I looked out the window again, the bike rider was walking up our path. She was carrying a clipboard. "Oh, for Pete's sake," I said. I knew the look, the intent, she could have been me.

I stood and went to the door and Humbug was bristling beside my leg. I figured I'd catch the seller before she made herself known.

"Hi!" she beamed at me as I snuck outside less than gracefully.

Here it comes, I thought, the pitch.

"I've been admiring your yard. It sure looks like you put a lot of work into it."

Textbook.

She went on, "Can I ask you though—do you ever feel a little overworked by it?"

"Let me guess," I said. "You're going to ask if I want to sell any of it."

"I—"

"You'll offer me a staggering amount just for that scratch in the dirt over there."

Her eyes narrowed, "Have I been here before?"

"No. You work for the Martian Bureau, right?"

Now her eyes widened. We weren't allowed to say the words.

I said, "It's okay. I work for them too." I pointed, "You've got a map at the back of that clipboard filling with dots."

"Oh," she said. "Isn't that funny? I'm sorry."

"It's alright."

"There's no way I could have known."

I agreed. I asked her what she thought of the Bureau. I listened as she explained her trouble. She was desperate to make quota. I didn't know we had one. She was in a real predicament. She said one more sale would put her over the top. A damsel in distress fairytale. Tried and true. Humbug barked in the window. I heard enough misery. I said fine. Mars wins again. I took her from the path, across the dew to the driveway and I drew a little square with the toe of my shoe. "Will that do?" I smiled in spite of myself. The shoe was on the other foot. So this is what it's like.

CHAPTER TWENTY-NINE
More Excitement

Thankfully, after that the street became a calm Sunday morning again. The birds were back in their places and the show must go on. I had a receipt in my back pocket and a hundred-dollar bill. I thought that would be all the excitement for a while.

And then the letter arrived.

I wasn't surprised it was a day late. They hired one of the saddest-looking delivery robots I've ever seen. It took it two days to reach our neighborhood.

I left my chair and off I went to the door. This time Humbug got past me, bounding down the steps into the yard.

The robot gimped along the sidewalk like a

goat slowly dragging its lunch of tin cans. It had been through the wringer. Humbug was barking on the fence, any second she might go airborne. The robot stopped at our gate and waited for me.

"Hi," I said. "You finally made it."

"Is this the right place?" It recited the address on the letter and lifted its spindly arm. "I got terrible lost getting here." It wore a compass like a wristwatch. The needle pointed North, then West, then jumped South. "I had to sleep in a alley last night."

I took the letter and opened the gate. "Come on in. Don't worry about the dog, she's all bark."

Humbug proved me wrong. She leaped at him and snapped his leg clean off. Down he went. I tried to push Humbug away, but she got under my arm and in a second she had the robot's leg in her mouth. "Humbug!" Too late, she gave a leap and flew straight up into the overhanging tree.

"Oh jeeze! I'm sorry." I got the robot balanced upright on one leg.

"S'okay. I got a bum leg. It's only held together with tape and a screw. It falls off all the time."

"Humbug! Bring that to me!" I whistled and stamped.

Nothing doing. The leaves churned. She wheezed that cartoon laugh.

The screen door banged. The kids ran outside to help. They were done watching in the house. Penny brought a box of dog biscuits and shook it. More excitement. And I didn't even open the letter yet. Wait until Shelley sees a ticket to Mars. Our house will blossom like Cape Kennedy.

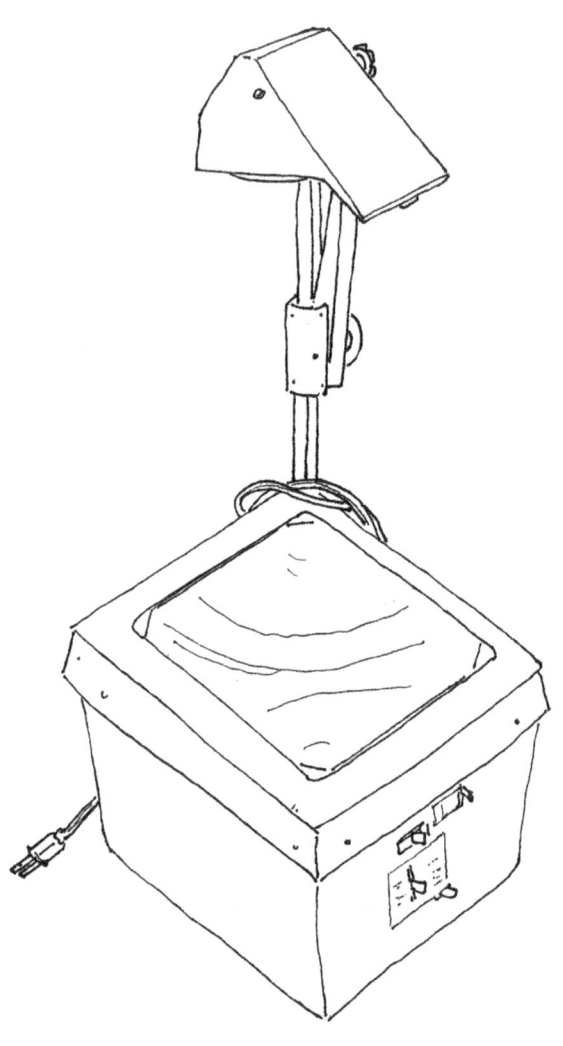

on the wall

CHAPTER THIRTY
With A Caterpillar

They weren't in the lobby with me, the family was finding our seats in the auditorium. I haven't been to the June on the Moon Children's Theater for a while. Red carpeting, wallpaper, arches, it felt like an old movie palace. Next to a poster of "Alice in Wonderland," I couldn't believe what was framed on the wall. My review for "The Princess and the Pea." It ended up in *The Wise Penny* shopper's gazette, page 24. Incredible! The pulp paper was turning sandy with age. I always wondered where it went. I read it twice. My words preserved in this temple. I bet I can get a copy. I've seen their newspaper office on the way to work. A basement lined with filing cabinets, full of the whole long history of *The Wise Penny* from its humble beginnings on a treadle printing press as big as a steam engine. Smalls towns were served and then bigger ones became cities like ours. Where would we be without *The Wise Penny*? I had a new appreciation. Funny, once in a while I pick one up at Food Giant, or I'll do the crossword at the laundromat in a plastic chair. I never knew I was a contributor. I laughed.

The girl guarding the curtained entry smiled. I said hi and showed her my ticket. She was dressed like a caterpillar. I didn't ask if she was in the play. Maybe she's waiting to be a butterfly. I didn't ask her if she read my review either. I didn't want to make a scene. Can you imagine? "Please…" I'd tell the theater crowd, "I didn't write anything that wasn't true. It was simply one of the most remarkable dramatic performances I've ever been witness to." That's not going to happen, don't worry.

A short, carpeted hall slanted upwards and sent me to a view of all the theater seats. There were a lot of people. I looked for my family. Some kids ran past me towards the stage. Way in the front row, Orville and Shelley waved at me. Penny fanned her program. They were all three laughing. I can tell why: they want to see me get picked from the audience. I have a history. They remembered "Peter Pan," when I got pulled up on stage by Captain Hook. They were still pleased with themselves as I sat beside Penny. I was so close to the stage I could reach out and play it like a piano.

My invitation materialized after ten minutes. The caterpillar was singing beside a painted cardboard castle. A crescendo of kids began to shout at a dragon tiptoeing onto stage. To them it was reality. The caterpillar looked woefully into the audience and begged someone out there to care. Everyone was waving and shouting, but it happened just as predicted, she pointed at me. I stood up and bowed. It was only fitting she wanted me. After all, I was a bit of a hero here.

I don't mind singing with a caterpillar and a paper mâché dragon. What do I have to lose?

CHAPTER THIRTY-ONE
A Little Jump

Anyway, that was a weekend with the Plentys. An eventful one. On Monday morning, the kids were out the door before me. I was looking for the keys, found them near the toaster. Shelley and Orville were standing in the driveway looking at the ground, examining the outlined red square of earth. "What is this?" Shelley asked. I had to be quick.

"It's ummm, yesterday a surveyor was here. She said they need to look at a pipe underground."

"I thought it was buried treasure," Orville said. He spun some story about pirates in the clouds who landed here last night and—

Shelley interrupted him, "Dad, I think I want to go to Mars in Spring."

"Well, that's good, but we need to talk more about it." I didn't make a scene about her speaking, not writing, sometimes she forgets, and honestly it was so nice to hear her voice.

"—and nobody saw them because we were all asleep," Orville continued.

I opened the cardboard car hatch for him and got him buckled in.

Shelley settled onto her seat. She explained, "You don't want to go to Mars during dust storm season."

"No way," I said. I opened my door and put my spaghetti leftovers on the dash.

Shelley wrinkled her nose. "Ughh! What is that?"

Orville laughed.

"It's my lunch. Cold spaghetti. The best." I started the car and the radio came on. It was an ad for Marvelous Marvin's Unreal Estate.

"—all kinds of deals for you right now. How would you like to find yourself living in a tropical paradise? That can be arranged! That can be installed for you today, for a very low, low price.

Come on over and see me this week and I'll give you two free dinners at Victoria Station."

Then static and the next spot on the dial. I tapped my hand on the steering wheel.

From the corner of my eye, I saw Shelley give a little jump. She unzipped her bag and grabbed her notebook and pen.

CHAPTER THIRTY-TWO
The Magic Word

I parked on Meridian Street in front of Olympia Pizza. I didn't cover the cardboard car, the sky didn't look like rain, it should be a good day for walking whatever neighborhood they assign me to.

An orange light was on in the back of Better Vacuums. Bernard was making his first pot of coffee.

I kicked a can away from the Bureau. It chattered off the curb. That's funny how that other seller came to our house. I wonder when she checks in for work. And Hector too. I haven't seen him lately. Are there more? Do they stagger us every hour? Every half hour? I've never tried to case the place, but it would be interesting to know. I don't plan on forming a union or a marching band, I'm just curious.

My code let me in. I walked on the sand in a murky room. I felt like that little diver in a pet shop aquarium, next to the treasure box with goldfish swimming around and bubbles when the box goes open and closed. "Good morning," I called.

The mist parted as I neared. A Martian sat at the table. No robot today. This was unusual.

H-E-L-L-O appeared above her. You got used to seeing floating words. It was like a Kurosawa movie. I remember when Shelley met her first Martian. She walked next to me holding my hand. Her other hand carried daisies. We were at the seashore. Martians get confused around water. This one was. Most Martians have never seen an ocean or lake. He was planted like a fencepost in the beach stones. A blurry single letter fizzled over him. I've seen this before. I knew he needed help. We're all warned on how to help a waterlogged Martian. We've all heard the announcements on the radio, seen the signs and warnings posted near fountains and rivers and reservoirs. I led Shelley over to him and we said the magic word that would revive him. Suddenly he was subtitles again and what a talker. Shelley reached her hands up trying to hold the words. If she could knock one down, she would bring it home in her pocket.

The Martian official took my clipboard. While she totaled and transcribed my sales updates, I looked around. Not much to see, although I guessed this was a simulation of a foggy Martian dawn. I wondered if they had an unreal estate agent do their decorating. Someone good like Marvin, not Charleston.

Her waving got my attention. I was caught off guard looking around the room and didn't realize there was a new sentence waiting in the air. "Sorry," I said, "I was daydreaming." I read the message and asked her, "I'm getting a new job? What is it?"

bean-counter

CHAPTER THIRTY-THREE
Sky On Water

Starting today I'm a bean-counter. I counted forty into a gunnysack. The Martian told me that was enough. Her goodbye dissolved and I set off. I'd be retracing my map at the back of my clipboard and planting beans where there were red dots. Not a bad job. I was a little scared at first. The office was spooky, she could have led me to count Sand-Bats in the tunnels below. Counting beans and planting them is preferable.

Outside, the Earth sunshine was welcome, telephone wires gleaming, sidewalk cement instead of sand. First, I stopped at the Asia Market next door and bought a steamed bun. Those don't grow on trees. Whistling a song that would last no longer than our jumpy radio fare, I returned to my car and saw the spaghetti on the dashboard. I smiled. I set the steamed bun next to it. The windshield was lined with treats like a buffet display.

I shut the hatch and got comfortable, put the bag on the seat next to me, leaned the clipboard against the steering wheel and flipped pages to the map. Hmmm, where to start…

The red dots formed a constellation. Not one that I recognized. A kid would draw a line connecting them, to reveal an elephant or a sailboat or something. That made the most sense to me, to draw a path like that, from where I am now to the end, counting down beans like a rocket launch.

Back where I started, I returned to Mill Avenue. That's where I bought the first bit of turf for Mars. Thirty-nine to go. Forty beans don't seem like a lot. I bet I could be done in a couple of hours. This was one of those jobs I could paddle at, take it easy like a canoe on a calm lake. I might stop for a while to stare into the reflection of the sky on water. The day would pass. Deep in the night the stars would arrange themselves.

CHAPTER THIRTY-FOUR
#34

In the gunnysack thirty-four beans remained. I also carried the triangle planting contraption. The Martian showed me how it works. It was easy, just put a bean in the slot at the top and touch the point to the ground. I was making good progress. Time has passed, seasons have changed since I was last in these places. Someone has been maintaining the plots so they match their surroundings seamlessly. The borders were red as the day I painted them.

#34 started as a shoeprint under an apple tree. I remember the old man who stamped it on that November morning. He took his payment to his house and shut the door. I didn't knock to let him know I was back. I didn't want to see him, once was enough, he wasn't the most welcoming sort.

So far nobody has noticed my reappearance, but if anyone has a problem, I'm just revisiting what is legally ours. I have the receipt in my clipboard, the Martians keep everything, they go by the book.

I settled on my knees beside #34. The apples above me were tempting, they were red and yellow and probably sweet and tart, the way I like them, but I resisted. I remembered the cold boot stomp the grass and the gnarled hand I stacked the twenties on. If he comes hobbling out waving a shillelagh, I don't want to be caught eating one of his apples. I quickly loaded a bean.

I say 'bean' but I don't know if that's really accurate. It could have been a bad translation I read in the air. It's not quite like any bean I've seen, larger than a pea, more like a marble.

The triangle clicked. You'd never know something was underground. There was no disturbance to the soil. I'm not sure what will happen when I try this on cement. I hope there isn't a ricochet. I'll find out.

An apple fell next to me. That was natural. They do that. It wasn't the only one on the ground either, it was September, they were falling the way they were meant to. I counted six other apples in the grass. I don't know how many more are ripe in the tree. That old man was their guardian, he knows every apple. I'm not the only one numbering things. The apple was tempting, but we can't just take things.

I picked myself up and carried on.

Besides, I wasn't hungry. When I was, there was food on the dashboard of my cardboard car.

so many stories

CHAPTER THIRTY-FIVE
Tulip

By the time I reached #27, I remembered how it was. It was my thirteenth dot on the map. I accepted what a strange job I had, and I was getting used to it. You could drive down Mill Avenue and never know what was in the backyard of an ordinary-looking house. There are so many stories hidden behind doors. This job showed me forty of them. I walked up the bumpy, weedy driveway, my shadow blued along the side of the wall past a window, into a row of tilting sunflowers, to a gate. A wooden sign on it read: Tulip. The fence must have been eight feet tall.

I know who Tulip is. I was surprised the first time though. When Virgil Chef told me how much he spends on food for his pet, I offered to help him out. We decided on a parcel in the corner of their backyard and I paid him enough for several months of Tulip welfare.

I rang the bell next to the gate. I waited to hear hooves and the gentle willow-like whoosh of breathing in the air. Even though I knew what I was waiting for, I knew I'd be surprised. I had my eyes fixed over the gate, twelve feet high where a face would appear. Tulip wasn't appearing. I rang the bell again and knocked. Nothing. Just the sounds of Mill Avenue.

The pickup truck wasn't in the driveway. Sometimes Virgil drives Tulip around in that. It was quite a sight, like the circus was in town. Maybe they went to the park. Oh well, I'd try to be quick. I loaded a bean and unlatched the gate.

No sign of any creatures. I crept onto the shadow of the big walnut tree and followed the branch silhouettes to the back fence. An airplane buzzed behind the leaves. Any leaves within Tulip's reach have been pulled down, whatever was left would be rusting soon enough and parachuting.

Red paint marked the spot. Paint? Was it paint? I never asked what the Martians have had me doing with all the land they bought— were they building a monopoly of backyards stretching like footprints across this city and beyond? That's possible. If that's true, they know what they're doing: there's a lot of struggling people and a lot of Martian money seems like a miracle you'd be crazy to reject. Especially for so little in return. I know the feeling. I'm no different, Mars owns some of our yard too.

CHAPTER THIRTY-SIX
Beans

Down to three beans took longer than I thought. More walking than I expected, also all that creeping around was exhausting on another level. The land belonged to Mars, but I still felt like some unwanted cloaked folktale menace up to no good, stealing my way through the neighborhood.

I spent ten minutes listening to #8 tell me about the hundred dollars I gave her for a square underneath the laundry line. Sheets were billowing around me. A blue sky between them. I was in their sails while I planted a bean. Her cotton shadow wanted me to buy more land from her. She had plenty she said. I told her I'm a farmer now, I'm not in sales anymore. That gave me a chance to say goodbye. Her voice trailed off. You don't see that many laundry lines, not in the city. It was nice, it was worth a hundred dollars to be there and remember the clothesline we had at home and what it's like to put on a shirt that's been dried in a sunny breeze.

I cut across a vacant lot and followed an alley toward Mill Avenue, half a block from my car. Almost there. A crow watched me from the top of a telephone pole. He knew about my lunch on the dashboard. Crows know everything going on. The kids and I think a lot about animals. Half of the books we read have talking animals. I wouldn't be surprised to hear the crow ask me, "Hey Mac, how about some of that food?"

A loud truck boiled down Mill while I waited to cross. Everly Dairy. It passed in front of me and then pulled over to the curb. A man in a white suit and cap left the milk truck and walked around to the bumper. As I crossed the street, I realized my circumstance sounds like that story about Jack and the Beanstalk, but in reverse. There I was with three beans—I was afraid he was going to open the delivery doors and there'd be a cow in back. I'd give him magic beans and he'd trade me the cow.

That didn't happen. He was just getting a

couple full baskets to deliver.

I'm not a character in a story, that's a relief. I smiled thinking about what would happen if I brought a cow home. Shelley and Orville would love it I bet. They'd be elated. I don't think Penny would be surprised to see me coming up the driveway with a cow. It would be fun to see their reactions, but what would we do with a cow? There wasn't much room in the backyard. If I left my cardboard car parked within reach, the cow might eat it. Or is it goats that do that?

The car was where I left it, safe and sound. I went around to the driver's door and got in. Only three beans left. I put the bag next to me and laid the clipboard on top. After lunch I would deliver the last beans by car. I was tired of walking. I unrolled the window and tore off a piece of bun to throw. I looked out the window and whistled. The crow was still watching me.

CHAPTER THIRTY-SEVEN
Loretta Lynn

While the car radio was jumping around, I heard that alert again: "Attention, if any unknown person attempts to purchase your property contact your nearest security official." It started to repeat. It was on a loop. Then we bumped and it was gone, the radio was Loretta Lynn.

What was that alert all about?

More songs followed. I was in a jukebox on wheels.

I got home early, before the piano was playing, and I parked. It wasn't going to rain, a clear sky over me, the car was fine in the driveway. The windchime Shelley made from spoons jangled lazily. The door burst open and Humbug rushed outside to greet me. Just like an Earth dog, she made it seem like she had been shipwrecked for years, waiting for me. "Hi Humbug!" I pet her as she spun. She whimpered and bounced and left the ground, turning cyclones in the air. What a greeting—if only the *Herald* was here to cover the drama.

"Hi dad!" Shelley called from the doorway.

"Hi!" I waved. "I'm just trying to get to the house!"

"I have some more thoughts about Mars."

I said, "Okay, Shelley. As soon as I get there." I staggered like an astronaut. Humbug nearly got hold of the gunnysack then she turned abruptly away from me, towards the driveway. "Humbug!" Where was she going? Right over to our hundred-dollar deed to Mars.

"Some lady was here," Shelley told me. "She was looking at that place too."

Humbug gave the spot a going over. She pawed at the dust.

"What's she doing?" Shelley said.

"I'm not sure…" I watched as her paws dug in and clawed a hole, tossing the raw soil behind her.

"Humbug!" Her head went down and she grabbed out what must have been the bean—if that lady had been planting them like me today.

I said, "I think she found a mole or something."

"Yuck!" That was enough for Shelley. She retreated inside the house.

"Humbug," I whispered, "Come here."

Humbug stared at me. The bean was in her mouth. She was telling me something. She crunched it and trotted down to the curb where she spit the remains into the road.

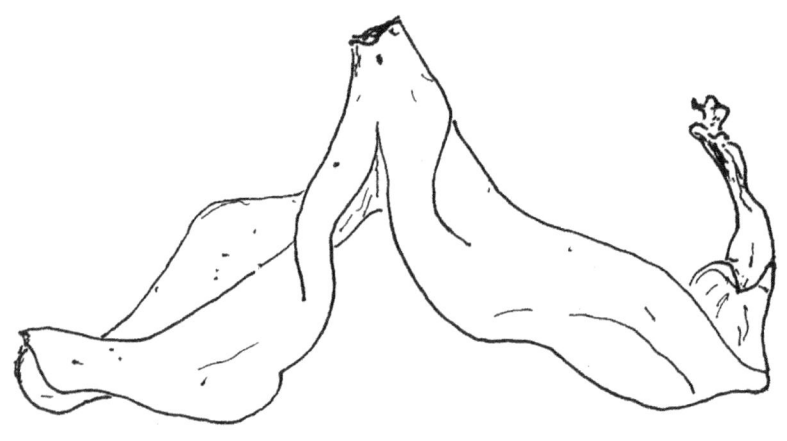

a fine way to fall

CHAPTER THIRTY-EIGHT
Driving A Jellyfish

The sound of rain woke me. Our bedroom was dark, the window was open, the curtain swelled with the cool breeze. At first, it was soothing. The rain was like a calm wet creature, like a giant seahorse nuzzling among the leaves out there in the tree. A whole herd of them were gently moving through the neighborhood. That would have been a fine way to fall back asleep, but then I remembered I left the cardboard car in the driveway.

"Oh gee..." I pulled the blanket off.

What happened to the uncloudy sunset? Rain was tucked out of sight. What nerve the sky had to decide to fool me like that. I got out of bed, leaving Penny asleep as I went down the stairs. Humbug lifted her head off the couch armrest, ears up, glinting eyes like coal. "It's okay," I whispered. "Stay there." In the kitchen I opened the door to the garage. Bare feet on the concrete.

I tried to be quiet tilting up the folding garage door so it slung overhead flat along the ceiling. Springs creaking in rusty annoyance with me. Light from the garage spilled over the driveway. Oh no, our poor cardboard car! It gleamed like a fish, its roof sagged and pooled, the rain had loosened its posture into a slump.

The gravel nipped my feet as I got hold of the bumper and began to pull it towards shelter. I had to use both hands. The rain went down the back of my neck. The wheels turned sluggishly, one of them was nearly square. A melted ice cream carton. I was soaked. Another half hour and I'd be driving a jellyfish to work.

I slung it to the floor inside. A splat like a net full of herring hitting the deck. My feet were cold, I was wet, Penny was in for a surprise when I got back into bed with her. I tilted the garage door down. My footprints slapped the cement. The car would be alright by morning. It would dry a little warped, that was okay.

Okay? The car was more than a little warped the next time I looked. I set my coffee down. I tried my best to smooth the dents and crumples, the door on my side didn't quite close, the tires needed air. The engine was a throaty rasp as we left the house. Hopefully it would run smoother once it warmed in the sunshine.

After the weather last night, the driveway held in the car's crooked mirror looked like a sunny postcard, backing up into California. The brake worked fine. I put us in forward gear. Shelley turned a dashboard dial and the radio coughed. It needed a moment to catch its breath then it repeated its warning: "Attention, if any unknown person attempts to purchase your property contact your nearest security official." At least that didn't refer to me. As I already said, I'm a farmer now.

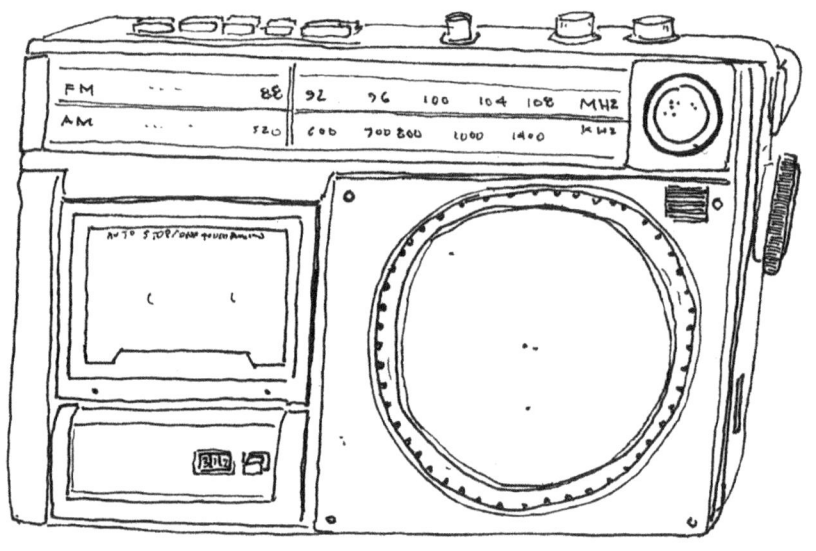

static and music

CHAPTER THIRTY-NINE
Magnified

By the time I dropped off Orville and Shelley at school, the radio had gone from one end of the dial to the other and then back to the station where it started: "Attention, if any unknown person attempts to purchase your property, contact your nearest security official...Attention, if any—"

Only one little voice on a radio full of other voices, static and music. Just someone with a transmitter and an aerial. Was anyone paying attention? Was anyone else wondering about the message?

If it was really important, the warning would be magnified, wouldn't it? Why hide it in my cardboard radio? If everyone needed to know, that voice would echo from a thousand radios, a fleet of speakers alerting all our citizens, anyone with a car and time to drive around, police sedans with megaphones, yellow taxicabs, metro buses, garbage trucks. The word would spread. The *Herald* would post headlines. There'd be sirens, running crowds, the tunnels would rumble with tanks and trucks, like a movie with a dinosaur on the loose. In a way, that would be easier to understand.

I couldn't help wondering if it was directed at me. I had been that unknown person buying land for Mars.

What's the problem anyway? We paid people. It wasn't a Martian invasion. It's all on the level. At any rate, they were too late with the radio message, Mars was done buying.

Weren't they?

There was no explanation from the robot at work and no word from the Martian woman either, just a new assignment, shuffling me like a poker card.

Cars stopped at a red light. Starlings sat on the wire watching it too. When it turned green, would they fly?

I needed to drop by the Bureau and get more

beans, but instead of turning on Holly Street and driving to Meridian, I kept going straight. It was a beautiful morning. I was free. I rolled my window down. Traffic swept along with me, other radios were playing, ones that stuck to a song all the way.

On my pothole radio, Marvelous Marvin promised a meadow in the Alps, a guaranteed lease with no credit check. It sounded too good to be true.

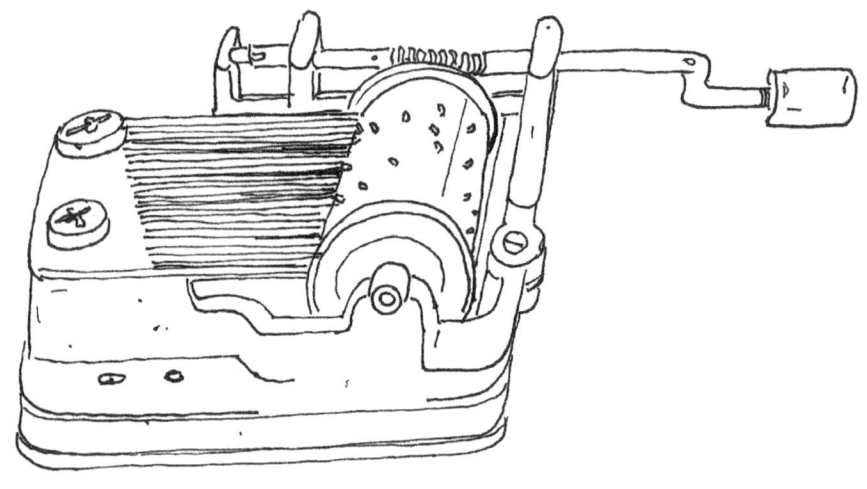

unseen machinery

CHAPTER FORTY
A Big Dream

Strange as it sounds, I've never gone to where Penny works. I mean, I've taken her here when the other car was in repair, I've seen her to the door. We kiss and I hurry away to the Bureau. Except for Saturday and Sunday—our days together—she goes to her work, I go to mine. So it goes in our modern America, there is hidden, unseen machinery that sweeps you up.

It's a story, from the first time we saw each other on the corner of Hawthorne Boulevard and 23rd, we never wanted to be apart. We found each other, that's what we wanted, love wrapped up in each other. We worked in the same place, I watched her glide, we held hands, the city was a big dream we shared together. I remember the mornings, days, and nights.

We built a nest, lined it with soft and precious things and we became a family. To care for it we go to-and-fro from the river and the shore and everywhere in between. During the day we disappear from each other, we separate to jobs or school, we're in different worlds. When we get home, we're a family.

Do we talk about tractors, protractors, or sewing machines? I try not to talk much about work. Mars made it clear, if anyone asks, I just say, "I'm in sales." Like Arthur Miller on the shoulder of a country road in the rain, a hundred miles from Wichita with a suitcase full of samples. The Martian Bureau wants it that way, they're from another planet, they have plans and secrets same as us.

I left the cardboard car next to another like it. This parking lot wouldn't make waves with The Parking Lot Appreciation Society. Not that such a society exists. Still, I'd like to believe Ruth is waiting for their calendar—she seemed to genuinely want that—she would pin it to the wall beside her desk and tell visitors about the morning their parking lot became famous. She didn't seem cut from the same cloth as Charleston Reese, I can still see her smiling and waving goodbye that day. You can usually tell by looking in someone's eyes.

My reflection got bigger in the glass door, then I pushed on it and went inside. The reception room was spare, a table, a few chairs, a shut door behind the table, a calendar on the wall. On the table was a typewriter and a phone, a green metal shelf full of paperwork, and a silver bell. I guess they didn't get much business. I took a few steps to the bell. The calendar caught my attention. The photo wasn't a parking lot, it looked like a place Humbug would love, the month of September in The Field Appreciation Society's calendar.

Penny opened the door before I had to ring the bell. It was funny to see her here, in a place I didn't know anything about, where she worked every day. She held me with one arm as we hugged, her other hand was around a cardboard shoebox. She put it on the desk, too close to the edge, and we both watched it fall in slow motion, hit the floor and when the lid flew off, Martian beans scattered across the blue carpeting.

CHAPTER FORTY-ONE
Candy

What would you do in this situation? I helped her gather them. They were just like the forty I planted yesterday. She closed the lid. I said I knew what they were, I told her I had an empty gunnysack in the car and I'm due to get more but I came to see her instead. She said wait right there. She carried the box beyond the door. From what I could see, a stairway going down.

It didn't take much imagination to picture the underground operation, rows of beans growing below bright lights. I was right, she told me about it when we went to the car for privacy. Her job was growing them.

I watched a blue jay. There was a cedar tree in the parking lot. When I spoke, I know I sounded like a drive-in movie star, "All this time, we didn't know we both work for Mars."

She laughed. Neither one of us could admit it until now. It's like the days we were working at the café together, only this time we go back and forth all day and never see each other.

The blue jay was gone. They're busy gathering food for winter. This one carried a cedar cone like a suitcase.

I didn't know what else to say. Why are we sworn to secrecy, was it a Martian plot, what are they worried about? Did it matter if we work for Mars or Pepsi-Cola?

Penny squeezed my hand. "I better get back. It's a lot to think about."

"I'll say."

She reached for the door hatch.

I touched her shoulder, "Oh, I forgot. I got you something at the Grocery Outlet."

She rolled her eyes. I know what she was thinking—more stale chocolate. No, I resisted that. It wasn't candy this time, it was something better. The store gets new things in all the time, you can't go there with a shopping list, they might not have what you need, but you can find something else. Like an apple grown on the moon. They had a display of them stacked on a pallet. Chalky-looking apples that came on a rocket ship. It's an amazing journey from the moon to here, landing at the cosmodrome, trucked to a boxcar, left on the rail unguarded at night where half of them will go missing for a black-market delivery. I bought two off the stack. One for each of us.

CHAPTER FORTY-TWO
A Rare Ability

The code didn't work. The door rattled, locked tight. I could picture that robot on the table inside. Neon grinning. Gradually putting its hands over its ears.

One last knock. I was late. That's probably why I couldn't get in. My code was overdue. Fine. I won't work today. No beans...I wondered about that Martian lady in there, I had some questions next time. I had a lot of them.

I was turning for the car when I spotted Hector approaching. He had his empty gunnysack balled in his hand. He recognized me, nodded.

"Door's locked," I told him. "My code won't work."

He grinned. "Same as last time."

"Only we switched places."

He asked me, "You on bean duty?"

"You too?"

He nodded. "Yesterday. I planted a hundred."

"Really?" That was impressive.

"How many you get?" he said.

"Ohh…" I said, "About a hundred too. I'm here to get more, but I can't get in."

Hector tried his code. Same thing. The door stayed locked. He tried it again.

"Did you get your balloon repaired?" I asked.

"No." He shook the door handle. Nothing doing. "I threw it away. I can live in cardboard for now."

"It's supposed to rain again."

Hector kicked the door. "What's wrong with the code?" Three times and the door wouldn't open.

I asked, "Is this your usual check-in time?"

"Yeah."

"Maybe they moved."

"Back to Mars?"

I shrugged. "I don't know what they're up to. Something strange is happening." I spun down some overgrown lane where the blackberry thorns were sharp as swords and dark bellowing creatures shook the leaves, where Mars was glowing large, orange as a jack-o-lantern up in the stars. Like children afraid of the dark, we turn to fairytales. You can believe anything if the shadows are right.

But the door opened, just half a foot, and the Martian was peering out. We were both surprised to see her. I hoped she wasn't listening to our conversation.

"Here's your beans," she directed Hector, passing him a new gunnysack.

"Thank you." He took the bag and gave her back his empty one.

Then she looked at me. Did she overhear me? I hoped she had a sense of humor. That seems a rare ability these days. Her words floated, "And here's yours."

"Ohhh," I said as I hefted it. "There's more than yesterday."

"It's *about a hundred*," she answered in tilted italic, smiled almost, then her words were crushed in the shutting door.

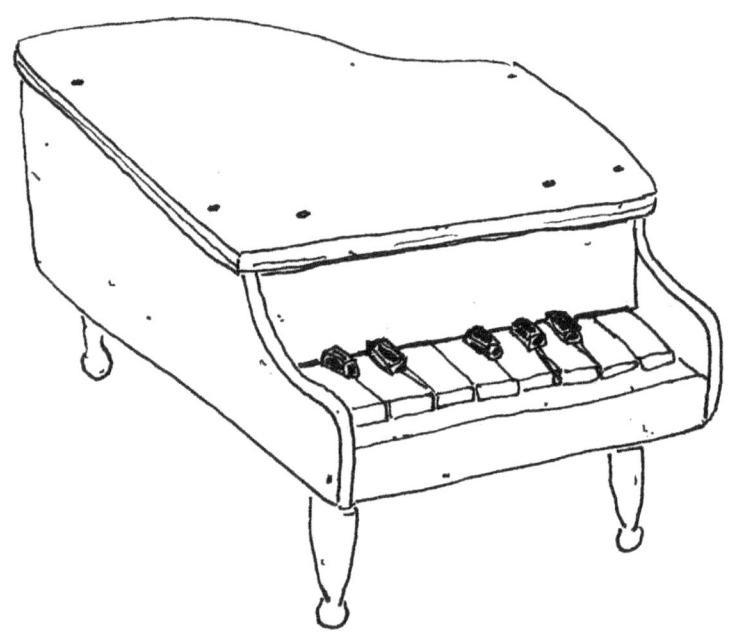

Fats Domino

CHAPTER FORTY-THREE
Laughs

Yes, she did have a sense of humor. Apparently that phenomenon translates to other planets. I could put a banana peel on a Martian sidewalk and get laughs. It doesn't need words held up like cue cards to explain comedy.

I sat in my car and counted the beans...98. Me and my big mouth..."*About a hundred.*"

From there, the day took hold of me and dragged me along. The sun went overhead. I was more than twice as tired as yesterday when I was done, holding onto the steering wheel like the Ancient Mariner. I got home as Fats Domino and his piano were bidding the corner goodnight. I drove past them. When I checked the rearview mirror, they were erased.

I got past our dog and waved hello and

stumbled to the couch where I fell asleep instantly. Drifting flotsam. I was too tired to dream, I was in a fogbank that rang with the clackety kitchen sounds of making spaghetti. I couldn't emerge, I was in that boiling pot with the pasta, as boneless as an octopus. Lost in that muddling underwater world, I was glad when Humbug put a cold wet nose on me and startled me awake. "Good dog," I mumbled.

As I turned on the cushion, my clipboard and gunnysack fell to the floor. Quick as you like, Humbug had the fiber bag in her mouth. 98 beans left their trace, one she didn't like at all. She gave the bag a fierce shake and bounded from me, growling, snapping it viciously.

Orville laughed and clapped and knocked over the candle. Penny was quick to catch it as the kids leaped from their chairs and ran from the table after Humbug. "That's Daddy's!" Shelley laughed. The three of them raced upstairs.

We could hear the kids shrieking, feet stomping, something falling. A chair? We were halfway up the stairs when they yelled from our bedroom., "Humbug! Humbug, come back!"

"What's happened?" Penny was a step ahead

of me. The kids were at our open window.

Orville pointed, "She escaped!"

"She flew into the tree," said Shelley.

"She still has the bag," Orville added.

"That's okay," I said. "There's nothing in it."

We were gathered around the window. Beyond our reach, the leaves were shaking where she hid, growling, standing on a branch in the dark thick of it. A torn scrap of the bag fell free.

"She's ripping it up!"

I told them, "That's alright."

Penny said, "I'll go get the biscuit box," and left.

Another smaller shred of the gunnysack drifted like a cinder, then another.

I could smell rain. Beyond the tree, the clouds looked like Orville's pirate dream sailing ships. Sunlight was losing, autumn was coming, and scraps of Martian cloth were falling leaves.

I got the picture. Martian dogs and those beans don't get along. I found out something else a Martian dog can do.

We heard the door open below and we saw Penny buzz along the path, shaking the box like a maraca.

CHAPTER FORTY-FOUR
Forever

Raining, raining, raining. Maybe I shouldn't have taken that nap. I was wide awake at midnight, staring at the ceiling, thinking in circles, listening to rain's radio static. Once we got the kids to bed, Penny and I talked about Mars until Orville knocked on our door.

He carried his windup radio into our room. Fiddles, banjo, the eerie harmonies about cold rivers, lonesome last words, unsleepy graves, ghosts who wander forever. His favorite station. For ten seconds. Then, like driving our cardboard car radio, he took us to the next station on the dial.

"Attention, if any unknown person attempts to purchase your property, contact your nearest security official." We've all heard that a few times.

Orville mimicked the announcer as the warning repeated and we laughed at his contorted serious face. What a hambone. After that performance, he bowed, said goodnight to us, bowed again and shut the door.

That was hours ago. It was the end of summer and this always happens, suddenly the wind and rain and cold return. Sunny days will become scarce. July and August were full of them and I could spend them like quarters in a jukebox. By November my pockets would be empty.

I couldn't sleep. I could have gone to the window, but what would I see? I couldn't see the moon and its apple fields—not tonight, too cloudy—in tomorrow's light I'd know what awaited.

When I looked at Wednesday morning, I'd think I was still dreaming. This is what I would see: The beanstalks are just like the cartoons predicted. Tall, as solid as redwood trees, reaching up beyond where we can see. They remind me of summer games we used to play, running in the garden like rabbits in the sunflower rows. The beanstalks are everywhere, sturdy as aqueducts. When I go to the Bureau, a stem grows right through it, so wide it pressed between the other stores. Roof tiles litter the pavement. Fifty feet up the leaves unfurl, wide as sails. A breeze rustles them and carries faint sounds down. That's where the Martians live, far above us. At night we see their neon and streetcar lights. Sometimes they ride to the ground and walk among us like angels. I'm ready to believe they're here to help. It's good to know good things can happen.

I yawned and turned over and put a hand on Penny. Her skin was warm. The rain was telling a long story, using the roof as typewriter paper. The story was about water that started in a cloud and as it fell from the sky, it turned into snow and landed on a mountain. It lived up there in a white field until summer warmed it up and let it run into a trickle, into a stream, into a river. It roared down through forest and farms and levees, past roads, under bridges. It became calmer as it flowed and reflected the clouds. Cows stood in it, fish swam in it, boats floated on it. Once it got to the city, the water wasn't clear, it brought all that it had been through to the ocean and mixed in. Something that was a snowflake was part of a much bigger thing. I shut my eyes. The rain tapped. All around the Earth went the water. It didn't float forever, after a while it rose back into the air when it evaporated and became cloud again. We used to draw that ritual on chalkboards in school. Rain is the water on a bicycle wheel. That hiss as you rode on tar, when you are almost home.

CHAPTER FORTY-FIVE
Ever-Present

I said, "You better look outside, kids! Wake up!"

"What is it?" Orville croaked. His blankets were balled up over him.

"Come on, look!"

I called to the next room, "Hey Shelley! Look outside!" while I snuck around some toys on the floor. The ceiling slanted over me. It's a steep roof. I've been up there a few times to cut overhanging branches, it's a dangerous stunt, next time I'm hiring a mountain goat. I pushed the curtains aside. The silver light of morning. Our ever-present neighborhood and oh, that's not all.

Orville rose up on his elbow. "What is it? Did it snow?"

That's usually the reason I'd be freeing the curtains like this at 7 AM.

He crawled from the covers and staggered with Penny to the window.

"Look," I whispered.

Before Orville could say a word, I heard Shelley sing out like a bird.

GOODWIN PLENTY
Writing: August—September 2024

AFTERWORD

That's one version of the story that girl told me on 24th Street. I was almost done writing this book. I was on a jet plane coming back from Maine. My parents were in the seats right in front of me. It was a long flight. The man sitting next to me was retired. He and his wife spend their lives on boats. There's no one river you could float on from the east coast to the west coast, they were taking the air to a cruise ship on the Pacific. Almost above Seattle, he reached into the seat-pocket and got a box of Good & Plenty licorice candy. That iconic box has been on my mind all summer! From the beginning I knew it would be this book's cover. So I took that apparition as a good sign, and I finished this book a few days after we landed.

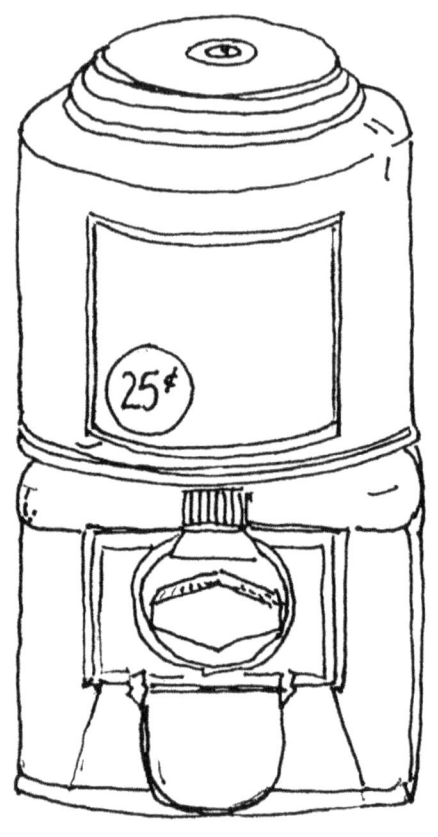

from *Ohio Time*, 2007

Books by Good Deed Rain

Saint Lemonade, Allen Frost, 2014. Two novels illustrated by the author in the manner of the old Big Little Books.

Playground, Allen Frost, 2014. Poems collected from seven years of chapbooks.

Roosevelt, Allen Frost, 2015. A Pacific Northwest novel set in July, 1942, when a boy and a girl search for a missing elephant. Illustrated throughout by Fred Sodt.

5 Novels, Allen Frost, 2015. Novels written over five years, featuring circus giants, clockwork animals, detectives and time travelers.

The Sylvan Moore Show, Allen Frost, 2015. A short story omnibus of 193 stories written over 30 years.

Town in a Cloud, Allen Frost, 2015. A three part book of poetry, written during the Bellingham rainy seasons of fall, winter, and spring.

A Flutter of Birds Passing Through Heaven: A Tribute to Robert Sund, 2016. Edited by Allen Frost and Paul Piper. The story of a legendary Ish River poet & artist.

At the Edge of America, Allen Frost, 2016. Two novels in one book blend time travel in a mythical poetic America.

Lake Erie Submarine, Allen Frost, 2016. A two week vacation in Ohio inspired these poems, illustrated by the author.

and Light, Paul Piper, 2016. Poetry written over three years. Illustrated with watercolors by Penny Piper.

The Book of Ticks, Allen Frost, 2017. A giant collection of 8 mysterious adventures featuring Phil Ticks. Illustrated throughout by Aaron Gunderson.

I Can Only Imagine, Allen Frost, 2017. Five adventures of love and heartbreak dreamed in an imaginary world. Cover & color illustrations by Annabelle Barrett.

The Orphanage of Abandoned Teenagers, Allen Frost, 2017. A fictional guide for teens and their parents. Illustrated by the author.

In the Valley of Mystic Light: An Oral History of the Skagit Valley Arts Scene, 2017. A comprehensive illustrated tribute. Edited by Claire Swedberg & Rita Hupy.

Different Planet, Allen Frost, 2017. Four science fiction adventures: reincarnation, robots, talking animals, outer space and clones. Cover & illustrations by Laura Vasyutynska.

Go with the Flow: A Tribute to Clyde Sanborn, 2018. Edited by Allen Frost. The life and art of a timeless river poet. In beautiful living color!

Homeless Sutra, Allen Frost, 2018. Four stories: Sylvan Moore, a flying monk, a water salesman, and a guardian rabbit.

The Lake Walker, Allen Frost 2018. A little novel set in black and white like one of those old European movies about death and life.

A Hundred Dreams Ago, Allen Frost, 2018. A winter book of poetry and prose. Illustrated by Aaron Gunderson.

Almost Animals, Allen Frost, 2018. A collection of linked stories, thinking about what makes us animals.

The Robotic Age, Allen Frost, 2018. A vaudeville magician and his faithful robot track down ghosts. Illustrated throughout by Aaron Gunderson.

Kennedy, Allen Frost, 2018. This sequel to *Roosevelt* is a coming-of-age fable set during two weeks in 1962 in a mythical Kennedyland. Illustrated throughout by Fred Sodt.

Fable, Allen Frost, 2018. There's something going on in this country and I can best relate it in fable: the parable of the rabbits, a bedtime story, and the diary of our trip to Ohio.

Elbows & Knees: Essays & Plays, Allen Frost, 2018. A thrilling collection of writing about some of my favorite subjects, from B-movies to Brautigan.

The Last Paper Stars, Allen Frost 2019. A trip back in time to the 20 year old mind of Frankenstein, and two other worlds of the future.

Walt Amherst is Awake, Allen Frost, 2019. The dreamlife of an office worker. Illustrated throughout by Aaron Gunderson.

When You Smile You Let in Light, Allen Frost, 2019. An atomic love story written by a 23 year old.

Pinocchio in America, Allen Frost, 2019. After 82 years buried underground, Pinocchio returns to life behind a car repair shop in America.

Taking Her Sides on Immortality, Robert Huff, 2019. The long awaited poetry collection from a local, nationally renowned master of words.

Florida, Allen Frost, 2019. Three days in Florida turned into a book of sunshine inspired stories.

Blue Anthem Wailing, Allen Frost, 2019. My first novel written in college is an apocalyptic, Old Testament race through American shadows while Amelia Earhart flies overhead.

The Welfare Office, Allen Frost, 2019. The animals go in and out of the office, leaving these stories as footprints.

Island Air, Allen Frost, 2019. A detective novel featuring haiku, a lost library book and streetsongs.

Imaginary Someone, Allen Frost, 2020. A fictional memoir featuring 45 years of inspirations and obstacles in the life of a writer.

Violet of the Silent Movies, Allen Frost, 2020. A collection of starry-eyed short story poems, illustrated by the author.

The Tin Can Telephone, Allen Frost, 2020. A childhood memory novel set in 1975 Seattle, illustrated by author like a coloring book.

Heaven Crayon, Allen Frost, 2020. How the author's first book *Ohio Trio* would look if printed as a Big Little Book. Illustrated by the author.

Old Salt, Allen Frost, 2020. Authors of a fake novel get chased by tigers. Illustrations by the author.

A Field of Cabbages, Allen Frost, 2020. The sequel to *The Robotic Age* finds our heroes in a race against time to save Sunny Jim's ghost. Illustrated by Aaron Gunderson.

River Road, Allen Frost, 2020. A paperboy delivers the news to a ghost town. Illustrated by the author.

The Puttering Marvel, Allen Frost, 2021. Eleven short stories with illustrations by the author.

Something Bright, Allen Frost, 2021. 106 short story poems walking with you from winter into spring. Illustrated by the author.

The Trillium Witch, Allen Frost, 2021. A detective novel about witches in the Pacific Northwest rain. Illustrated by the author.

Cosmonaut, Allen Frost, 2021. Yuri Gagarin stars in this novel that follows his rocket landing in an American town. Midnight jazz, folk music, mystery and sorcery. Illustrated by the author.

Thriftstore Madonna, Allen Frost, 2021. 124 summer story poems. Illustrated by the author.

Half a Giraffe, Allen Frost, 2021. A magical novel about a counterfeiter and his unusual, beloved pet. Illustrated by the author.

Lexington Brown & The Pond Projector, Allen Frost, 2022. An underwater invention takes three friends through time. Illustrated by Aaron Gunderson.

The Robert Huck Museum, Allen Frost, 2022. The artist's life story told in photographs, woodcuts, paintings, prints and drawings.

Mrs. Magnusson & Friends, Allen Frost, 2022. A collection of 13 stories featuring mystery and magic and ginkgo leaves.

Magic Island, Allen Frost, 2022. There's a memory machine in this magic novel that takes us to college.

A Red Leaf Boat, Allen Frost, 2022. Inspired by Japan, this book of 142 poems is the result of walking in autumn.

Forest & Field, Allen Frost, 2022. 117 forest and field recordings made during the summer months, ending with a lullaby.

The Wires and Circuits of Earth, Allen Frost, 2022. 11 stories from a train station pulp magazine.

The Air Over Paris, Allen Frost, 2023. This novel reveals the truth about semi-sentient speedbumps from Mars.

Neptunalia, Allen Frost, 2023. A movie-novel for Neptune, featuring mystery in a Counterfeit Reality machine. Illustrated by Aaron Gunderson.

The Worrys, Allen Frost, 2023. A family of weasels look for a better life and get it. Illustrated by Tai Vugia.

American Mantra, Allen Frost, 2023. The future needs poetry to sleep at night. Only one man and one woman can save the world. Illustrated by Robert Huck.

One Drop in the Milky Way, Allen Frost, 2023. A novel about retiring, with a little help from a skeleton and Abraham Lincoln.

Follow Your Friend, Allen Frost, 2023. A collection of animals from sewn, stapled, and printed books spanning 34 years of writing.

Holograms from Mars, Allen Frost, 2024. Married Martians try to make do on Earth in this illustrated novel.

The Belateds, Allen Frost, 2024. The Belateds came to Seattle in 1964 and left the four chapters in this novel.

Jones Jr., Allen Frost, 2024. If you're a fan of 1970s television detectives, you'll be at home with this yarn.

Flop, Allen Frost, 2024. The B Minus Gallery presents a timeless work of art, while a seal goes out with the tide and pterodactyls spin in the sky.

Goodwin Plenty, Allen Frost, 2025. An illustrated novel about Mars buying backyards. Let's look in on the Plentys and see what happens.

Books by Bottom Dog Press

Ohio Trio, Allen Frost, 2001. Three short novels written in magic fields and small towns of Ohio. Reprinted as *Heaven Crayon* in 2020.

Bowl of Water, Allen Frost, 2004. Poetry. From the glass factory to when you wake up.

Another Life, Allen Frost, 2007. Poetry. From the last Ohio morning to the early bird.

Home Recordings, Allen Frost, 2009. Poetry. Dream machinery, filming Caruso, benign time travel.

The Mermaid Translation, Allen Frost, 2010. A bathysphere novel with Philip Marlowe.

Selected Correspondence of Kenneth Patchen, Edited by Larry Smith and Allen Frost, 2012. Amazing artist letters.

The Wonderful Stupid Man, Allen Frost, 2012. Short stories go from Aristotle's first car to the 500 dollar fool.

Your cashier was CANDY
Thank you for letting me serve you!

www.ingramcontent.com/pod-product-compliance
Lightning Source LLC
LaVergne TN
LVHW061046070526
838201LV00074B/5201